# TEARS ON FROZEN GROUND

## A STORY OF JINCY
## 1815-1863

# TEARS ON FROZEN GROUND

## A STORY OF JINCY
## 1815-1863

Gale Maag

Tears on Frozen Ground
A Story of Jincy 1815-1863

Print Edition | September 2019
Copyright 2018 by Gale Maag
Cover Design by Lolly Walter
Cover Art by Ramona Yates

All Rights Reserved. This book or any portion thereof may not be reproduced or used in any manner whatsoever without the express written permission of the author except for the use of brief quotations in a book review.

This book tells a story about real people who lived in the 19th century. While Jincy, Caleb, and their family are real, and the story contains factual elements, at its heart this is a story that pieces together a family's oral history with the author's imagination. It is not intended to be perceived as wholly factual.

Printed in the United States of America
First Printing, 2019

ISBN 978-0-9997133-5-8

Awl Collaborative Press
PO Box 2435
Pflugerville, TX 78691

Awlcollaborativepress.com

*This book is dedicated to the many descendants of Caleb and Jincy Bales, both far and near. To all who have ties to the Bales, Craig, Harness, Marshall and Morris families that we proudly claim in our family history. And with special significance, to my children, grandchildren, nieces and nephews, who all share a connection to their grandmother and my mom, Hester Roena Bales Maag (1901-1998).*

# Table of Contents

Foreword ................................................................ xi
Preface .................................................................. 3
Part I  Background and History ............................. 7
Part II   The History of the Craig Family ............... 15
Part III  Caleb Meets Jincy ..................................... 29
    Indian Territory ............................................... 31
    Cherokee Maidens ........................................... 35
    The Valley of the Spring .................................. 39
    On the Trail Home ........................................... 45
Notes ................................................................... 79
Epilogue .............................................................. 81
Acknowledgements .............................................
About the Author ................................................

# Editor's Note

My grandpa told the best stories. The sillier and more far-fetched the better. And he told them with such sincerity that to this day, I don't know which ones were real. He didn't tell us the story of Jincy, though.

I don't know whether he didn't know the story, or whether he thought it was too mature for little ears. I'll never find out. He died the summer before my senior year of high school. I've missed him for a very long time now.

But reading Jincy's story, the result of my Uncle Gale's research and his imagination, I feel that connection with Grandpa. After all, the story is his, too. I also want it to belong to my children and my grandchildren, if I am blessed enough to have some one day.

I want them to know they are descended from a strong, brave woman who survived some of the cruelest treatment young America inflicted upon the children of this continent. Uncle Gale has given us all a gift by reminding us of both a past failure of our nation and the indomitable spirit of our family, from Jincy to my own grandpa, to my children.

Lolly (Maag) Walter<br>Austin, TX   2019

# Foreword

*"My friends, circumstances render it impossible that you can flourish in the midst of a civilized community."*
—President Andrew Jackson in an 1835 message to the Cherokee Nation

All my life I have heard stories of our Native American ancestors. My father, Charles Maag and my grandma, Hester Bales Maag, sometimes, but rarely, spoke of our Cherokee roots. Grandma was a little more descriptive than Dad, but neither gave any real details on the matter. Grandma Maag said that there was blood from the Cherokee in her background. She explained they didn't talk much about this because being an Indian was not well-accepted by society. By the time she told me what little of our background that she did, there were fewer taboos left regarding Native American lineage. The stigma of being seen as a half-breed had been much more serious during her upbringing.

Great Grandma Margaret Angeline Bales would tell a tale of a great journey that a member of our family was forced to take. She said many did not live through the trek. She also stated that our great-great-grandmother couldn't wear shoes because of the damage done to her feet during the march while walking on the frozen ground barefoot. Grandma Margaret said this grandmother did not have any shoes and that they walked a long way and cried many tears. I was only five years old when she told these stories, and I certainly had no idea what the Trail of Tears was, but her tragic tale stuck with me as I grew up.

## Foreword

I don't know why, but history made sense to me at a very young age. Grandma's information led me on a quest for more knowledge, and I stored every tidbit away like a squirrel for winter. Every time I watched a western movie, I wondered if my family had been on the other side!

I remember Dad telling me the same story that Grandma Margaret Bales had told about the grandmother who could not wear shoes because of her journey over frozen ground, and I asked him her name. He didn't know, so I asked Grandma Maag. She said her name was Jane, and that her husband's name was Caleb. I assumed that these were the parents of Great-Grandma Margaret. I continued to believe this into adulthood.

I asked Grandma Maag what her dad's name was, and she told me that her father's name was James Allen Bales. She said he was named after his father James Bales Sr. I asked her many questions about her family over the years. She told me she was raised in an area north of Batesville, Arkansas called Weavers Chapel, and that her dad was a schoolteacher who loved art and, of all things, calligraphy! I could never coax her into revealing any more about her native roots.

I recall one incident that happened over fifty years ago with Grandma Maag that did not make sense to me, until I researched more on the history of Indian removal from native lands. I had been on a trip to Tennessee, and we had taken a detour to visit Andrew Jackson's home, the Hermitage. Upon returning, I went to Grandma's apartment for a visit. She was eager to hear all about my trip, but when I told her about our excursion to the Hermitage, she frowned and said, "That old criminal. I wouldn't waste my time to see anything he had to do with."

Needless to say, I was taken back by this comment, but when I asked her why she would make such a statement, she just smiled and changed the subject. Anyone who knew her knew you might as well move on, because when she was done talking about something, it was over! Also, anyone who knew our grandma knew she was a kind and gentle lady who never said a cross word about anyone. Many years later, the reason behind her disdain for President Andrew

# Foreword

Jackson became clear when I found that he had signed the order forcing the Indians to move from their beloved lands to the new territory in Oklahoma.

Years passed, and so did our beloved Grandma Maag. So much history has been lost with the death of those who lived it. After her death, I tried multiple avenues to find out about our Cherokee roots, but to no avail. In 1998, and since I live nearby in Tulsa, Oklahoma, I went to the Cherokee Center at Tahlequah, Oklahoma to search for clues. Tahlequah became the capital of the Cherokee Nation soon after their arrival following the Trail of Tears. I found nothing! I did, however, learn that anyone searching for his or her Indian ancestry is fighting an uphill battle. You have practically no chance of finding useful information unless you have a decent oral history or your ancestors are listed on an Indian census such as the Dawes Roll. Accurate records were not kept by government agencies during removal or even before, because the Native American people were not considered citizens. They had no rights under the laws of the day. My only hope was to find enough oral history to piece together the story fragments of Great-Grandma Margaret, Grandma Maag, and my dad. That hope was realized when I stumbled upon documents placed on the internet by two descendants of Jincy Craig and Caleb Bales—Celia Bales Comer and Idella Haltom. Celia was the last of nine children belonging to Cynthia Jane "Jincy" Craig and Caleb Bales. Idella Haltom was the granddaughter of Jincy and Caleb through their fourth child, Dianna Bales Comer.

I had always believed that our Indian roots came strictly from Great-Grandma Margaret Marshall Bales, since she was the one who had told the stories about the journey. Now, this information piqued my interest even more, and I could see to my surprise where the Trail of Tears saga came from—James Allen Bales's side of the family!

Celia's story is a touch disjointed, probably due to the stress of her reason for writing it down. She was working to receive recognition as a member of the Cherokee tribe. Celia was rejected. No one she listed as a family member was to be found on any of the Indian rolls, so the government, along with the tribe itself,

# Foreword

disqualified her claim. Unfortunately, this was the usual outcome of these types of claims. This is not proof against her being Cherokee, only that the claims board did not find sufficient data to prove it. Since Indian money and land was involved, the commission was not liberal with their approval.

Idella's story could be the "fill in the holes" answer to many of our questions about what happened. After living in "Indian Territory" for thirty years, I am very aware that many Native Americans have this type of oral history, and they take it very seriously. What follows is Idella's story, "Notes from My Memory."

There are many unanswered questions, and we will probably never have all the answers. Maybe we will find more clues along the way, even clues to our elusive great-grandma Margaret Marshall Bales' background. There is a strong Indian tie there too. Nevertheless, there is no doubt we are Cherokee!

Diane Frie<br>
Tulsa, Oklahoma, 2017

Foreword

*Above: Isabell Bales, the last child born to Jincy and Caleb. She lived most of her life in the Oklahoma Indian Territory. I wonder how much this pretty lady favored her mother, Jincy Right: John Benjamin Franklin Bales, son of Jincy and Caleb.*

*In the above picture, with his family, you can see the handsome features of John Benjamin Franklin Bales, seated front left. I expect his father Caleb also had these features.*

xv

# Notes from My Memory

*I do not claim these statements to be factual, but things my Grandmother related to me during my growing up years. Signed, Idella Williams-Haltom, Tahlequah, OK.*

*Grandmother Mary Comer Ives was very proud of her Indian ancestry, (Jincy Jane Craig) and often told us of the hardships and mistreatment the Indians suffered at the hand of white men as they were forced from their homes.*

*The Craig Family was a prosperous farming family whose large farm was situated on the North Carolina and Georgia state line. The Indians were peaceful; many of them owned large tracts of land and owned slaves, at the time the government decided to remove them to the reservation (1830's).*

*They resisted and the Indian Leaders took the blood oath swearing they would die before they would consent to selling their land and being removed to a strange new land.*

*As time dragged on, land speculators moved in, creating fear among the Indians threatening them, and offering to buy their land. It was at this time, some of the Cherokee leaders betrayed their people, and they disregarded the blood oath they had taken and sold their land to white men and moved on to Oklahoma.*

*John Craig and his son had gone to a fort for supplies and when they didn't return at the appointed time, his young son went in search of them. He found them the following day murdered near their freight wagon, which had been looted of supplies and horses.*

*Since Indians had no recourse in the courts of laws, and were looked upon as being less than human, it was counted as robbery and nothing was done to find the killers and bring them to justice.*

*Sometime later, a white man came to advise John Craig's Wife, Modare Harlan-Craig, and her Children to move off the land. He (the White Man) produced a deed dated the day of Jim Craig's death and had witnesses (white men) and proof that he had bought and paid Jim Craig for said land. The*

## Foreword

*remaining Craig Family members put up much resistance, but to no avail, the white man had the deed and the land was his. However, it was near harvest time and the crops were good he agreed to allow the Craig Family a part of the harvest, which never came? (Illegible).*

*Just a short while later, when the Craig family was seated for the evening meal, the sound of horses and shouting broke upon the peaceful scene, men surrounded the house beating upon the doors making demands ordering the family to march out into the herd telling them only "you are going to the reservation." They allowed them only what belongings they could hurriedly gather up and carry on their backs. There was much chaos as the men on horseback herded the livestock down the lane ahead of them.*

*Before leaving, the men ransacked the house taking whatever had value, before setting fire to the house and barn.*

*Jincy Jane Craig, the pretty nineteen year old daughter, shed many tears through her life time as she related the incidents of those horrible days to her children and grandchildren. The Trail of Tears became a lifetime of tears to Jincy Jane.*

*As darkness fell, they continued to march on. At last, near daybreak they reach a camp where they were assigned to an overseer, a man named Jason Phelps. He was a cruel man who had no regard for the old and the sick. He made the same demands on everyone, regardless of condition.*

*The Cherokees were given just enough food to keep them alive and were made to sleep on the ground, many without blankets. They were kept in the camp for several days until Mr. Phelps quota for the march was met (several hundred). At last they were ready to begin the long trek to an unknown land.*

*On and on, day after day, they were herded along the trail for as many miles as they could walk. Only the very sick and old people were given horses to ride from one camp to the next.*

*Many of the sick children and older people died along the trail. They were not even given a burial, only covered with bush and leaves, and left for the animals to devour. Such was the fate of Jincy Jane's Mother (Modare Harlan-Craig), who died from exposure to the cold winter. She was left alongside the trail, covered with brush and leaves near the Mississippi river.*

*The weather was very harsh as they marched across Arkansas. By the time they reached Batesville (Arkansas) many were sick, supplies were gone, they were forced to make camp at Miller's creek just outside of Batesville.*

# Foreword

*Grandmother often showed me the place of the camp as we were going into Batesville. There was no bridge there until much later, only a shallow place when buggies and wagons crossed the Creek. It was here at the fort where the Indians camped.*

*At this juncture, all the cattle had been butchered and the supplies exhausted. Mr. Phelps asked the farmers for assistance in feeding and caring for the hungry, sick Indians.*

*The Bales family, one of the most prosperous farm families who owned a large farm what is now Weaver's Chapel responded.*

*Young Caleb Bales was sent to deal with Mr. Phelps to solicit a man and woman to work on the Bales farm. Instead of a husband and wife, Mr. Phelps assigned a brother and sister, Jincy Jane Craig and her Brother (James Granville Craig); thus Caleb and Jincy Jane met. The beautiful dark haired maiden was very happy on the Bales farm.*

*Soon she and young Caleb were in love. When the time came for the unscrupulous Mr. Phelps to continue the march to Oklahoma, Caleb made a deal with him and Jincy was permitted to stay on with the Bales family, where she and Caleb were married. They lived a happy life as they raised a family on the Bales homestead.*

*Notes:*

*Jincy Jane's Brother, James Granville Craig, chose to go on with the march to Oklahoma in search of his sweetheart who had gone before them in the earlier removal. Jincy Jane never again heard from her Brother, but later his descendants were located in Tahlequah, Oklahoma.*

*Jincy Jane could never wear shoes as her feet were badly crippled due to walking barefoot on the hard frosty ground.*

*Jincy Jane Craig was an educated woman for her day in time. In her early years, she attended mission school which the church had set up for them in earlier times. She fit into the community, taught neighboring children to read and write, since there was no school at the time.*

*She often said "I don't know how much I'm worth, for Caleb never told me how much, or with what, he bribed Mr. Phelps for my Freedom."*

# Tears on Frozen Ground
A Story of Jincy 1815-1863

# Preface

How fortunate we are that the great-granddaughter of Jincy Jane Craig Bales left us this "Note from My Memory." And then again, that the great-great-great-granddaughter of Jincy, Diane Maag Frie, found this letter on the Internet several years ago.

As Idella Williams-Haltom pointed out at the beginning, the stories from her letter were not completely factual, but they still hold many important clues concerning our heritage. Idella told the story as best she could remember. That story had been orally passed down from Jincy to Mary Comer to Idella's mother. Idella recorded this bit of history, some sixty years later, as best she could from her memory. How grateful we are.

In fact, Jincy and Caleb were living in their cabin near Weavers Chapel in 1838 when the Captain Benge party of Cherokees came through Batesville on the "Trail of Tears." It was already known along the frontier that the Cherokee were being forced west, and it became known around Batesville that a group was coming through the area. Jincy had to have known about these, her people, on the trail just a short distance from her home. She also would have wanted to visit with these Indians and gather any information they might have. She heard the stories of the round-up in the eastern states and the harsh treatment of these Cherokee at the compound sites situated throughout their homeland.

She would have known exactly where they camped at the creek going into Batesville. She would also have talked to her granddaughter about the struggles of her people on this journey. This could easily have been misconstrued to mean that Jincy was actually in that group, when she was not. She came over in 1833, five years before this group. Jincy would also have her first child in April of 1839, four months after the event here. The notes from Idella led us to further understanding, and from there we researched to learn even more. Without her notes, even with their inherent inaccuracies borne from being passed down orally for so many years, we might still be guessing about some vital facts. Thank you, Idella.

Because the Cherokee had no recourse with the law of Georgia, there are no records of the death of John Craig, Jincy's father. We will accept what we think is a fact: that he was murdered along with his son. We also can accept that they were forced off the family farm near Red Clay, as so many were. This fact is well documented, leaving Modare with no choice but to get to the new territory with her four children.

I find no record of Lieutenant Phelps coming through Arkansas. There was a Lieutenant John Phelps serving in the roundup of Cherokee that took place in Georgia, North Carolina, and Tennessee in 1838. Lt. Phelps was a disciplined soldier, and he followed orders even if he did not like them. His name could easily have been remembered by the Cherokee who visited with Jincy in 1838. The memory of the roundup would still have been vivid in their minds.

Phelps was, in fact, assigned a group to escort west into the territory; however, before these orders were enacted, they were rescinded by General Winfield Scott because of the very hot conditions and the general bad health of so many Indians at this time. Lt. Phelps received new orders that took him northeast. He later became a general in the Civil War and much can be found in his journals. He also wrote daily journals about the treatment of Cherokee Indians during the time when he was with them in 1838. His journals and history can be found throughout the historical record. I use the name Lieutenant Phillips later, simply because it was similar to this name in "Notes from My Memory."

If the Captain requested help from the surrounding community to feed and shelter these Indians for a short time during the winter in 1838, I expect Caleb and Jincy would have certainly helped. This could explain the story of young Caleb Bales being sent to get workers for the farm. At this time (1838), Caleb and Jincy were the only Bales known in those parts. They would likely have taken in two Cherokees.

As the Caleb and Jincy Bales family grew, they would later become large landowners in the Weavers Chapel area, with several hundred acres of land.

There is no question that Idella left us bits of valuable information in this letter. Just knowing where they camped at Batesville gives us an opportunity to see the actual crossing site, and yes, it is underneath the North Main Street Bridge, just a short distance from downtown Batesville, and on the exact route that Caleb and Jincy would have used any time they went to town.

Our family has always been very close. Hester (mom) was the one who instilled in us the love and closeness we all have for each other to this day. She was severely burned when she was three years old by the fire her mother had made under a wash kettle in the front yard of the original James A. Bales home just north of Batesville, Arkansas. Grandmother Margaret quickly smothered out the flames with her hands but not before Hester was scarred for life.

Hester could not walk on her own without a crutch until she was ten years old. At the age of nine she began a strenuous stretching exercise program, on her own, to rehabilitate her badly scarred right side. Standing in front of a mirror she charged ahead with determination to overcome the pulled, warped stature of her body. Soon she began to see the results of her determination as her body slowly began to straighten, and she was able to walk in a more normal manner. Until her death in 1998, she walked with a slightly curved stature, bent toward the side where she was scarred, a very distinct walk.

She overcame this tragedy through determination and a willingness to make all things better. Hester was an optimist. She prayed her way through life, especially the tough stuff. This was the way she coped, remembering the good, putting into perspective the bad, and recognizing the present can chart paths never dreamed possible. She instilled this quality in all her children and somewhere down deep in our souls, this personality trait seeps outward, even today.

Thinking about where this unique temperament originated takes me back to the times when my people on Hester's side of the family endured great difficulties. It was in the 1820s and 1830s that the lives of my Native American ancestors were to be changed forever. A time when families had absolutely nothing but the family itself to go forward with; everything seemed lost and only the healthiest and most determined would survive. Death lurked all around. If they were not burying their own, they were burying friends, often in shallow graves and sometimes just covering them as best they could with leaves and branches as they were forced on their way.

Here is some history behind the story of *Nunna daul Tsuny*, the trail where they cried.

# Part I

# Background and History

## Timeline of the Cherokee Removal

Around the turn of the 18th century, the new American government encouraged the Cherokee to end their traditional way of life and take up acceptable Christian American practices in life, farming, and religious worship. At the same time, many Americans moved to the South in search of land. Native Americans were seen as impediments to white expansion into territory that would become Georgia, Tennessee, Alabama, and Mississippi.

After the Louisiana Purchase in 1803, President Thomas Jefferson suggested that eastern Native tribes should be moved west, to the far side of the Mississippi River, where they could have their own space and more gradually be assimilated into the white way of life. Most Cherokee didn't want to move, preferring to stay on their own land and in familiar, established surroundings. Some groups, though, took up President Jefferson's offer and settled in the area of the Arkansas and White Rivers.

Meanwhile, the persecution of the eastern tribes continued. The state of Georgia held eight lotteries where they gave white men land already belonging to the Cherokee and the Creek. One of many treaties between Native tribes and the government, the Treaty of Cherokee Agency, established in 1817, provided land in the West for some Cherokee at the expense of Cherokee lands in the South, which helped to strengthen a growing rift between groups who wished to stay in their ancestral homes and those who wanted to take what the United States government was offering and leave.

Most of the Cherokee tried to prevent their land from being seized. They adopted the suggested behaviors that made them seem more like white people. They converted to Christianity. In 1827, they wrote their own constitution and enacted a government modeled on that of the United Sates. Their efforts were not enough for the American government, who continued to allow states and individuals to make aggressive attempts to seize Cherokee land.

The United States government offered promises and provisions. According to the 1828 Treaty of Washington, for example, Natives moving to western territories were guaranteed compensation for their land, a rifle, a blanket per family member, a kettle, food and provisions while traveling, and one year's provisions after reaching the Indian Territory. Offers like this became the basis by which America forcibly removed Native groups.

Also in 1828, white settlers became aware of the presence of gold on Cherokee lands in Georgia. In the ensuing rush for gold, the state pressured President James Monroe to remove the Cherokee. He told Congress that all Native Americans should be removed to the land west of the Mississippi River. In Georgia, the Cherokee were beset with robbers and trespassers and had no recourse. According to the Wednesday, May 27, 1829 edition of the *Cherokee Phoenix and Indians' Advocate*:

> Our neighbors who regard no law, or pay no respect to the laws of humanity, are now reaping a plentiful harvest by the law of Georgia, which declares that no Indian shall be a party in any court created by the laws or constitution of that state. These neighbors come over the line, and take

the cattle belonging to the Cherokees. The Cherokees go in pursuit of their property, but all that they can effect is, to see their cattle snugly kept in the lots of these robbers. We are an abused people. If we can *receive no redress*, we can feel deeply the injustice done to our rights.

In 1830, Congress authorized the Indian Removal Act, which was put in place to allow states to seize lands belonging to Native tribes. In return, all Native people were to be removed to an equal land west of the Mississippi. Again, the government agreed pay for the relocation and provide some assistance to Native people as they acclimated to the new land.

After a series of setbacks in the Supreme Court, which ruled under Chief Justice John Marshall that Native tribes were sovereign and not beholden to state laws, President Andrew Jackson said, "The Chief Justice John Marshall has made his ruling; now let him enforce it. He then agreed to forcibly remove all eastern tribes from their land.

The 1835 Treaty of New Echota established a two-year window for the voluntary emigration of the Cherokee people. Many Cherokee had not wanted the treaty and refused to move. In 1838, the remaining Cherokee were forced on an 800-mile march to the Indian Territory. In May, General Winfield Scott, who oversaw the removal of the Cherokee during that time, addressed them directly.

## Orders No. 25 ~ Gen. Winfield Scott's Proclamation to the Cherokee People, May 10th 1838

Cherokees! The President of the United States has sent me with a powerful army, to cause you, in obedience to the treaty of 1835 [the Treaty of New Echota], to join that part of your people who have already established in prosperity on the other side of the Mississippi. Unhappily, the two years which were allowed for the purpose, you have suffered to pass away without following, and without making any preparation to follow; and now, or by the time that this solemn address shall reach your distant settlements, the emigration must be commenced in haste, but I hope without disorder. I have no power, by granting a farther delay, to correct the error that you have committed. The full moon of May is already on the wane; and before another shall have passed away, every Cherokee man, woman and child in those states must be in motion to join their brethren in the far West.

My friends! This is no sudden determination on the part of the President, whom you and I must now obey. By the treaty, the emigration was to have been completed on or before the 23rd of this month; and the President has constantly kept you warned, during the two years allowed, through all his officers and agents in this country, that the treaty would be enforced.

I am come to carry out that determination. My troops already occupy many positions in the country that you are to abandon, and thousands and thousands are approaching from every quarter, to render resistance and escape alike hopeless. All those troops, regular and militia, are your friends. Receive them and confide in them as such. Obey them when they tell you that you can remain no longer in this country. Soldiers are as kind-hearted as brave, and the desire of every one of us is to execute our painful duty in mercy. We are commanded by the President to act towards you in that spirit, and much is also the wish of the whole people of America.

Chiefs, head-men and warriors! Will you then, by resistance, compel us to resort to arms? God forbid! Or will you, by flight, seek to hid yourselves in mountains and forests, and thus oblige us to hunt you down? Remember that, in pursuit, it may be impossible to avoid conflicts. The blood of the white man or the blood of the red man may be spilt, and, if spilt, however accidentally, it may be impossible for the discreet and humane among you, or among us, to prevent a general war and carnage.

Think of this, my Cherokee brethren! I am an old warrior, and have been present at many a scene of slaughter, but spare me, I beseech you, the horror of witnessing the destruction of the Cherokees.

Do not, I invite you, even wait for the close approach of the troops; but make such preparations for emigration as you can and hasten to this place, to Ross's Landing or to Gunter's Landing, where you all will be received in kindness by officers selected for the purpose. You will find food for all and clothing for the destitute at either of those places, and thence at your ease and in comfort be transported to your new homes, according to the terms of the treaty.

This is the address of a warrior to warriors. May his entreaties by kindly received and may the God of both prosper the Americans and Cherokees and preserve them long in peace and friendship with each other!

Rarely mentioned in the history of Batesville, Arkansas is the fact that these multitudes of Native Americans actually came through the town at all. Perhaps their relocation in large numbers was such a common scene in those days that it was not even worth a mention in Batesville history.

# Part II

# The History of the Craig Family

Understanding the living conditions of the Cherokee in the 1830s and the way of life they were being stripped of is essential to understanding the Craig family of the Red Clay area and why they gave up and moved west.

Historians have tried to describe the conditions of these oppressed people for close to two hundred years, and none of the descriptions can accurately portray the deplorable treatment they suffered. The best way to understand the horrible conditions under which they were living is to study the proclamations made by the people themselves, focusing closely on the words of the individuals and reading between the lines to understand how they were suffering. They were beaten down, much like a wild stallion would be to ready him for the plow, into complete submission to the authority of the one with the whip. They were led into the unknown with no hope of anything other than a handout of grain at the end of the day, feeling nothing to live for and never knowing where the next step might lead.

This "trail where they cried" began several years before it became known as such. Our ancestor Jincy no doubt arrived in Arkansas with a group of Indians under armed guard. These early departures of Cherokees were looked upon in disgust by other groups under the influence of Chief John Ross. They needed armed guards on the trail to protect them from their own people. Ross's leadership was to resist relocation in hopes of government intervention, protection, and entitlement to the land that was actually already theirs. A very successful leader of the Cherokee Nation, John Ridge, spent years traveling back and forth to Washington, meeting with legislators, presidents, and others who had influence, trying to find a solution to the invasion of the whites on the Cherokee homeland.

Ridge, from a prominent family within the Cherokee Nation in Georgia, had gone to Connecticut as a young man to study at the Foreign Mission School. While there, he met and married New Englander Sarah Bird Northup. In 1825, after Ridge and his wife returned to New Echota, he was named to the Cherokee National Council and became a leader in the tribe, thus beginning his work to save the land belonging to the Cherokee.

At last Ridge saw no suitable resolve for their worsening situation; he and his people were beaten to the ground. The only way to achieve any semblance of peace and happiness was to agree to removal and start over, even though Chief Ross led his Cherokee nation in vigorous opposition of any such action. Heavily burdened, Ridge and a small group of his people finally agreed to the Treaty of 1835.

The Treaty of New Echota was originally signed on December 29, 1835, in New Echota, Georgia by officials of the United States government and representatives of a minority Cherokee political faction, the Treaty Party. The treaty established terms under which the entire Cherokee Nation ceded its territory in the southeast and agreed to move west to the Indian Territory. Although the treaty was not approved by the Cherokee National Council or signed by Principal Chief John Ross, it was amended and ratified by the U.S. Senate in March 1836, becoming the legal basis for the forcible removal known as the Trail of Tears.

Only a few thousand Cherokee left for the territory at this time in 1835 and 1836, with government protection and provisions. Ridge was among them. They arrived in the territory of Fort Gibson, Oklahoma, and endured only minimal hardships during their trip. Little did the thousands and thousands left behind know of the suffering to follow during the forced removal of 1838, as evidenced by the following Cherokee plea:

### Petition of Cherokee leaders from the Aquohee Camp to General Winfield Scott, Fort Cass, June 11, 1838

> We your prisoners wish to speak to you. We wish to speak humbly for we cannot help ourselves. We have been made prisoners by your men, but we do not fight against you. We have never done you any harm. Sir, we ask you to hear us. We have been told we are to be sent off by boat immediately. Sir, will you listen to your prisoners. We are Indians. Our wives and children are Indians and some people do not pity Indians. But if we are Indians we have hearts that feel. We do not want to see our wives and children die. We do not want to die ourselves and leave them widows and orphans. We are in trouble. Sir, our hearts are very heavy. The darkness of the night is before us. We have no hope unless you will help us. We do not ask you to let us go free from being your prisoners, unless it should please yourself. But we ask that you will not send us down the river at this time of the year. If you do we shall die, our wives will die or our children will die. Sir, our hearts are heavy, very heavy... We cannot make a talk, our hearts are too full of sorrow. This is all we say...

Major Ridge, his son, and his son-in-law all signed their death warrant when they agreed to this treaty and moved to the territory in 1835-36, and they all knew it. In the year of 1839, the three of them were murdered on the same day, in different locations of the new Indian territory of northeast Oklahoma and just a few months after the arrival of Chief John Ross and thousands of other Cherokee in the winter of 1838–1839.

Later descendants of our own Jincy Jane Craig Bales petitioned the Cherokee Nation for admittance to the western tribe. All requests were denied on the grounds that John Craig, who was their connection to the eastern tribe before removal, was not a part of the removal rolls of deported Indians and that he did not attend council meetings in the old homeland.

They might have made it simpler by stating that he was of the early group that traded Cherokee land for land in the territory, an act that was viewed as treason by the tribes of Chief John Ross. Executions were carried out for this action in the early removal times, as well as later, in the Indian territory.

Earlier treaties gave these Cherokees some incentives to move west, well ahead of the New Echota treaty of 1835. The Treaty of Washington in 1828 was offered with several promises from the government to escort these Cherokee west and trade land for land, give kettles, blankets and rifles as well as one year of food upon arrival in the new territory. The pressure from the whites and state governments made life unbearable for these people to stay in their native homeland. The Trail of Tears actually began several years before 1838 when it became known as such. Jincy definitely came over with an early group in 1833.

It's difficult for us to comprehend the vast numbers of Indians east of the Great River who were forced to migrate into Arkansas and Oklahoma during the first half of the nineteenth century. Thousands were pushed west, all coming through Arkansas. Indians were not an uncommon sight anywhere in Arkansas—and they came at all times of the year, usually in small groups, but sometimes in larger numbers. Once into the foothills of the Ozarks, they might travel with purpose, and then at times, they would settle into a community of earlier removal parties and become part of a community such as Wileys Cove, Arkansas, now known as Leslie. This is the place where my great-grandfather James K. Marshall met and married my great-grandmother Jane Harness Marshall, and it was also the place of birth of my beautiful grandmother Margaret Angeline Marshall in 1878. Wileys Cove was an Indian village, a known fact among historians in Searcy County today.

When we look at the census of these communities in the 1840s through the 1860s, we see that these Indians are listed as "white" by the census takers. They had established themselves in the white community by way of land claims they had with the government (land for land). They had titles to the land in the form of a deed, and they were taxpayers. Only home and landowners were listed on a census. The censuses were taken in homes throughout the region, and anyone who owned property was included and counted as a white farmer and a taxpayer. Anyone in a household who wasn't black was counted as white, sometimes as a boarder or as a sister, brother, aunt, uncle, mother, father, or a stepchild and always as white. They were often noted as having been born in the eastern states of Tennessee, Georgia, North Carolina, Mississippi, and Alabama, with only the young ones counted as having been born in Arkansas. It is sometimes possible to tell when a family came to reside in Arkansas just by looking at the birthplaces and ages of the children—the younger ones born in Arkansas and the older ones born in the land east of the Great River. I have noticed how most of the adult people living at Wileys Cove were actually from Tennessee. Not all, but most were, an indication that these Indians tried to stay together as they moved across and beyond the Great River.

It is interesting how these Indians were listed as white people on the census of those days. Listing them as white was easy, as they had become a part of the white culture, with land and homes, adopting Western dress and appearance. They had been convinced years before to give up their "wild ways," to become "civilized" and mesh with the white community. Brutal treatment in the past, for no other reason than that Indian blood flowed in their veins, made most of these Cherokee wish to lose the identity of "Indian." They still did not trust the white man's promises.

In other instances in Arkansas, Indians were not landowners. They could be found living in the hills with huts for homes or roaming land that they did not own. These Indians were not listed on the census rolls – they were nomads.

Like my grandmother Margaret Angeline Marshall, these people began to mix in with the white people. For example, in the city of Batesville, Arkansas, they might appear slightly Indian, especially to the white folks who had seen so many Indians come across the state over the years. The locals had an eye for people of color, even a diminished color. This population of Indians was quickly recognized by local whites as "breeds" in these new surroundings. Most were of mixed blood and were more difficult to identify than a full-blood, since they no longer wore Indian clothes. They had, for the most part, taken on the white man's appearance while living in the hills and mountains of Tennessee, Georgia, and North Carolina, before coming west. However, the white members of the community often expressed prejudice at town gatherings, even though they might be standing right next to an Indian and not realize it. In groups or gatherings, even church, the Native American residents would overhear comments about the Indians who lived nearby. Indians were considered to be on the same level as the black slave people—and sometimes even lower.

In 2012, while discussing directions with an old farmer west of Batesville, my son Stan Maag, grandson Ben Adams, and I heard an old man say, "Which was worse, the nigger or the Indian?" This was one hundred and eighty years after Caleb and Jincy lived nearby, and one hundred and fifty years after my Grandmother Margaret's time. What must it have been like in their days?

We see when looking at the family of Caleb Bales and his Cherokee wife, Jincy Jane, that several of their children moved west to the Indian Territory after they were grown. They wanted to be around their own people rather than the whites in their community of Independence County, Arkansas. They preferred to meet future husbands and wives in an area where they were surrounded by people of their own ethnicity, and no one talked about breeds in a derogatory manner.

Most of our family had long thought that most of our Native American blood came from the Marshall side of the family. We had not heard much of Caleb Bales and his wife Jincy Jane and their Indian connection. We have mistakenly believed that Margaret A. Bales's mother, Jane Morris Harness Marshall, was the main influence of Indian blood.

We began to search and found that James K. Marshall was most likely Indian and was reported to have come to Arkansas with his mother, who was as much as three-quarters Cherokee.

James K. married into strong Indian blood with his first marriage to Anna Watts, whose family can be traced to Cherokee in Georgia and Tennessee in older days. He had also settled around Wileys Cove at the time of this marriage. Wileys Cove was known as an Indian settlement in 1830. In the 1870 census James K. listed his place of birth as Cherokee. With this information we can all see a possible connection with the Cherokee thru the Marshall side of the family.

I don't recall ever hearing anything from my mother or her sibling's side of the family suggesting that Jane was Indian. However, we could not find her. She showed up on the census as the wife of John Harness. After his death 1869, she married James K. Marshall. After James K. died in 1897, we see where she transferred her land to her sons and then disappeared.

We searched thousands of census records in Searcy, Van Buren, and Independence counties in north central Arkansas. Then we searched records in Washington County in northwest Arkansas. Nowhere could we find our great-grandmother. We did not know where she came from previous to her marriage to John Harness or where she went after the death of her second husband, James K. Marshall.

Now in our modern times and with the help of DNA we can see that some assumptions we made have no support as being accurate. Jane Harness Marshall has been searched by many in our extended Bales family as well as many in other families but with no confirmed evidence of her ancestry. Now with new DNA technology, the results are astounding.

Several years ago, my daughter Jennifer bought and sent to me a DNA test from Ancestry. I allowed this test kit to sit around for more than a year. Then one day I ran across it in a stash of old items that had been completely forgotten in a drawer. I opened the test kit and followed the directions inside and mailed it to Ancestry. A few weeks later my test came back with more information than I could absorb. A few months later Jennifer picked up on it on our Ancestry page and began a search thru DNA. Just recently she has found some remarkable facts about our Jane Morris Harness Marshall, my great-grandmother.

She found that I have fourteen DNA connections to Robert Morris, Senator from Pennsylvania and signer of the Declaration of Independence in 1775, through Jane Morris Harness Marshall. This has a long way to go before it can be confirmed and will require patience and persistence. I will leave this study and research to others who may be interested.

For some unknown reason the Harness family that was so dear to Margaret A. were never acquainted with her Bales family. Neither my mother Hester Bales nor any of her siblings remember ever knowing Jane, their grandmother. She never came to their home for a visit. They all have passed down stories of Grandmother Margaret going to visit the Harness family during the early years of their lives. Grandma would simply leave and be gone for a few days from time to time. It was always thought that she was visiting with her mother and the Harness family somewhere not too far from Batesville, Arkansas. Grandma Margaret was born to James K. Marshall and Jane at Wileys Cove on August 17th, 1877.

Jane was about sixty-four years old when James K. died in 1897. She was healthy and strong and had never known anything but hard work all her life. And she likely left the area to find work. Jean Sykes and I had a conversation about this in 2012 in Hot Springs. Jean described conversations she'd had with Grandmother Margaret when Margaret lived in a little one-room house beside the Sykes family in Hot Springs. Jean was a young teenage girl at the time and only a few steps outside her own front door was her grandmother's house. She loved her grandmother and would visit with her daily. It was on one of these visits that Grandmother Margaret shared a bit of information about her mother, one of the few bits of information we grandchildren ever received. Grandmother revealed that later in life, her mother, Jane, had gone to a lumber or sawmill operation for work, not far outside Independence County. And that was it. Jean gained nothing more except that her great-grandmother Jane had, in her older years, worked at a sawmill. The day Jean told me about this conversation was a moment in life that I will never forget. It was also the last face-to-face conversation I had with Jean, although I talked to her occasionally on the phone until her death in 2013.

On a visit to Batesville in 2014 with my nieces Jamie Fowler and Judy Owens, we visited the city museum. There inside the museum were pictures of Guion, Arkansas and the great timber operation that existed there at the turn of the twentieth century. Only a short trip up the White River from Batesville (a two- to three-hour boat ride) was perhaps the largest timber operation ever in Arkansas among many similar operations in the privately-owned timber industry. Employment could easily be found there; it was a likely place for Jane Harness Marshall to have traveled to after James K. Marshall's death.

Grandmother Bales always kept in touch with this family and even carried pictures of some of them. I have in my possession a picture of my grandmother's nephew, Warnie Harness, which she kept in her little overnight bag. I still have the bag and some of its contents. Nephews and nieces hold a special place in the hearts of aunts and uncles, and this well-dressed young man, Warnie, had a special place in the heart of his Aunt Margaret—he was her brother's son.

I also have a tag from a spray of red roses sent to Margaret's funeral from "The Harness Family" at the time of her death in 1958. The red rose in general symbolizes beauty, passion, courage, and respect. This "Harness family" had all these feelings toward Margaret.

Sometime around 1956, I drove Mom, Aunt Virgie, and Uncle Clarence "Squirrel" Danner to meet Grandmother Margaret and Uncle Raymond Bales at Cave City for a visit to their old home on

Cave Creek Road, as well as to other places around the area. I don't recall that we went to the Caleb Bales site as we know it now. I am sure we visited with some old folks in the area at that time, but I can't recall who. I do recall Mom, Aunt Virgie, and Uncle Raymond discussing the land and money they felt like they were still owed. I did not understand exactly why they felt they were owed land; however, later in discussion with my cousins Jean and Jo Sykes, I began to understand from them that they were speaking of the fact that the family had been denied admission into the Indian Nation. Their parents and grandparents had petitioned for admission into the Cherokee Nation at the end of the nineteenth century. This petition was to the Dawes Commission of Cherokee Indians at Tahlequah, Oklahoma.

This petition was a much-discussed subject in the lives of all the Bales families at that time and for years after. There had been a mountain of work to do to get ready to go before this Indian Nation Council. Lawyers were hired, depositions were gathered from everywhere imaginable and from those who could vouch for the Bales family and the Craigs, Jincy's family. It undoubtedly took months to prepare, perhaps years. It was a subject of conversation for the duration of this fact-finding time period and then for years to come. Notarized documents of all the Bales' and Craigs' petitions for admittance into the Cherokee Nation are on file in the courts of Independence County, Arkansas.

I am sure that Margaret and her son Raymond Bales visited Shirley, Arkansas on their return home to Hot Springs. She would insist on going by to visit with her kin, the "Harness Family." They must have had a great visit there with family she held so dear in her heart. She most likely stayed a day or two

Tears on Frozen Ground

*Above (l to r): In the front row are Grandmother Margaret, Aunt Dorothy, and Hester. In the back row are Uncle Ted, Aunt Grace, Aunt Virgie and Uncle Roy. Taken around 1955. Above, right: My beautiful grandmother, Margaret Angeline Marshall Bales. She was named after her grandmother, Margaret A. Morris, who was Jane's mother. Below: Grandmother Margaret and five of her children, 1955.*

Ted, Raymond, Roy Bales-Virgie Danner, Margaret Bales, Hester Maag

27

Gale Maag

*Above: The old Morris homestead, built in 1849, as photographed by Mary Jane Morris in 1949, 100 years after it was built. Right: Mary Jane Morris was the niece of Jane, our grandmother, and daughter of D. Henderson Morris, who was a brother to our Jane. Mary traveled from Idaho to Arkansas in 1949 to visit the old home place.*

# Part III

# Caleb Meets Jincy

# History and Our Family

# Indian Territory

In 1832, Fort Gibson was the central site, or headquarters, of the Indian Territory. This is where the Indians went to find the help and support promised by the U.S. government for their settlement in the west after their removal from their eastern homelands.

Our own Caleb Bales served for one year, from 1832 to 1833, under the command of Captain Jessie Bean's mounted Rangers. Captain Bean was a neighbor of Caleb Bales in Independence County, Arkansas in 1830 when the first census of that county was taken.

In 1832, Congress approved President Jackson's request to put six hundred mounted Rangers on the Indian frontier to fight Indian wars and also help make peace between the tribes in the new Indian

Territory who were at war with each other. Caleb and several of his friends packed their horses and joined these Rangers, eager for a new adventure on the frontier. The U.S. government would pay them one dollar a day and furnish them with rifles and a sidearm, along with provisions and feed for themselves and their horses. They departed for the territory of Oklahoma in August 1832. There were approximately one hundred and twenty officers and enlisted men in this company of Rangers. They would all arrive at Fort Gibson, Oklahoma Territory in September 1832.

The first assignment handed down to this band of young Rangers was a thirty-day tour of the prairie. A commissioner of the government, Henry L. Ellsworth, was sent to the fort to accompany this group on the tour and also take a message to the Indian chiefs that the President of the United States of America wished them to make a treaty with each other. Ellsworth also wanted them to visit Fort Gibson for the treaty talks and to receive gifts from the great American Chief, the President.

En route to Fort Gibson, Mr. Ellsworth met Washington Irving, a famous author, and invited him along on the journey. Irving accepted his invitation and traveled to Fort Gibson to join the Rangers of Bean's company for the tour of the prairie. He made notes and daily entries in his journal that covered the miles of frontier that was unknown to the white man. This journal would later become a famous book, *A Tour of the Prairie*. (This great book is available to read for free on the internet.)

At times when the troops were back safe at their quarters at Fort Gibson, they would join in the social life of dances and feasts, which included invited guests in the territory. An invitation to this event was a prized possession. All who received invitations readily attended these gala events.

### The Social Life at Fort Gibson in the 1830s

Excerpted from the Oklahoma Historical Society's *"Chronicles of Oklahoma,"* volume 2, no. 2 June 1924, by Grant Forman

Fort Gibson became the centre of such social life as the wilderness afforded; trappers assembling at the trading post nearby to barter their packs of beaver and buffalo skins, and passing traders going to Santa Fe and Mexico stopped to visit at the garrison and requited the hospitality they found there with tales of adventure and strange people. Busy little river steamboats brought visitors and news from the outside world. Social amenities were observed within their rude limitations, dinner parties in the log quarters of the officers sat around bountiful tables of wild provender—turkey, buffalo, bear, wild fowl, and wild honey became commonplace.

Gaiety and pleasure were not impossible, and the tedium of garrison life far from civilization was relieved by dances and gatherings graced by feminine loveliness from near and far. Beside the daughters and wives resident at the garrison, charming and accomplished maidens of the Cherokee tribe, some of them educated in eastern schools, formed part of the social life at Fort Gibson. Propinquity and charm— romance nurtured by the sylvan surroundings on the banks of beautiful Grand River—led to many happy marriages between officers and enlisted men and Cherokee girls.

Even from far away Fort Smith and other Arkansas towns, daughters of the early settlers regarded an invitation to a dance or a visit at Fort Gibson as an outstanding event. One related to an appreciative granddaughter how, as a girl before the Civil War, she rode horseback the ninety miles from Fort Smith carrying in her saddle bags the evening frock she had worked on so hard with visions of the alluring picture she was to make before handsome young officers at Fort Gibson.

## Cherokee Maidens

The dances and feasts brought the unmarried Cherokee women to the fort, and they were a favorite interest of the Rangers who made up the military population at Fort Gibson. The Cherokee women were beautiful, well dressed, and anxious to meet and capture a handsome military husband, one with whom they could have a family.

    They had been told to strive for blending throughout their lives, as the Cherokee in North Carolina, Tennessee, and Georgia adapted to the white man's ways. The government had for years encouraged them to become a part of the white society—a must if they were to flourish among a white community. They had attended mission school, and some had even gone to eastern colleges. They learned the English language and practiced it in their homes with their parents and other siblings. They learned to read, write, and excel at math.

These were the type of Cherokee women and young girls who were invited to these social affairs. Young officers and enlisted men took notice of the Cherokee maidens. Many of these men would settle nearby and make their homes on land granted to them by the government, a bonus for their time served.

Our own Caleb Bales was a private in this First Ranger Company to arrive at Fort Gibson, Oklahoma Territory in the fall of 1832. Caleb later received an eighty-acre land grant in Independence County, Arkansas for time served with Jessie Bean's Rangers. These Rangers were described as rough, tough, and honorable men by Washington Irving in *A Tour of the Prairie*.

The young officers and enlisted men were all eager to serve on the frontier, many having little to their names back where they came from in Arkansas. They began to look for property to homestead and then began to seriously look at these beautiful Cherokee maidens who were accustomed to the frontier kind of life. It seemed a perfect fit for these wild, young, handsome men to marry a pretty Cherokee and begin a family in the beautiful open country of the Grand River. After all, back east they were encouraged to seek their fortune in the West, to "Go west, young man, go west."

They saw and heard it everywhere. It was printed in all the daily newspapers. Others were settling by the thousands on the cheap land east of the Mississippi. Here they were in a land west of the Mississippi few white men had ever seen, and that land was plentiful. Even before they were discharged, many were taking Cherokee wives who were eager to live in huts, tents, or whatever they could find and wait for their new soldier husbands to take them away to a homestead. To the young frontiersman planning his future, having the good fortune of finding a Cherokee woman or girl was almost too good to be true.

Around this time, Caleb was twenty-seven years old. He had been on his own for years. He could provide well for a wife and family in the hills north of Batesville, Arkansas. He was seriously taking in all the courting and marrying going on at Fort Gibson in the summer of 1833. He had talked to the officers and enlisted men and heard their conversations about how good their Cherokee wives were—how hard they worked, cooked, and kept house in a hastily built log hut, and made do until their husbands' enlistments were over. Most of these young Cherokee women had been through tough times back east in their homeland and on the trail getting to the Indian Nation. These tough women, accustomed to very few finer things, would be happy just to have hope for a future with family and children. They worked and made a good impression while waiting for their new husbands.

As his discharge date, August 21, 1833, approached, Caleb had still not had an opportunity to find and enter into a courtship with a future wife. He was a patient man, and that patience had been displayed years earlier when he had searched northern Independence County for just the right place to homestead.

Independence County had a population of two thousand people in 1828 when he made his choice of a homestead. Caleb came to Batesville on a riverboat up the White River. He had left Virginia a few months before and patiently traveled west. The entire country was talking about all the free land west of the great river.

# The Valley of the Spring

Vaughn Brokaw, a descendant of Caleb and Jincy Bales and a distant cousin of mine, still lives on the original Bales property just west of Weavers Chapel. On a recent visit with Vaughn, he told me emphatically that Caleb Bales came up Polk Bayou to find the property he homesteaded in 1828.

In the hot summer of 1828, Caleb was observing the clear, cool water emptying into Polk Bayou. He drank from the stream and knew immediately it carried cold, sweet spring water from the valley from which it flowed. It was summertime, and the coolness of the water pointed the way to the thing all frontiersmen must have—an endless supply of fresh water. Traveling two or three miles up this brook, Caleb watched and checked the water supply in the small creek as he went along. The farther he went up the valley, the more convinced he was that he would soon find his destination–the spring from which this water flowed.

Caleb had chosen to hike the country to look for the perfect homestead site. He had packed up a burro with everything he might need. Walking would keep him connected to the land. He had decided to use the burro at the last minute. It was also half the price of a horse, and burros were dependable.

A few miles up the valley, the small brook made a big swing toward the east, and some open meadow appeared. Caleb could see the brook outlined with cottonwood trees hugging the south side of the valley. The water had slowed to a small, constant stream, and then it stopped completely. Caleb was now above the spring. He had not noticed the cold water coming from the rock in the bottom of the creek bed. Retracing his steps, he quickly recognized the very point of the continuous supply of cold water. A pool just below the spout of the spring was about six inches deep and held as much water as needed for a cool bath. Shallow water escaped over the next rock and then moved on downstream toward Polk Bayou, the creek Caleb had followed out of the trading post from its mouth at the White River. This brook had pointed the way to the source of the spring and what was to become Caleb's homestead, a place he could start and raise a family.

He staked his claim then and there, a simple stake that would make this beautiful valley his and his children's for years to come. He loved his discovery. At this time, Caleb was twenty-one years old. A year earlier, when he left Loudoun County, Virginia, his thoughts had been on the exciting adventure ahead. He had heard many stories about the opportunities for the future in the west. He was now there and liked what he saw.

The wilderness he lived in was developing slowly. Little developments, like a trail that went east from the valley he lived in to Weavers Chapel, and then from there to other small settlements such as Cave City and Batesville. In the other direction, the trail went to Sand Town and on to Cushman and then Melbourne. Caleb's little valley would soon have daily travelers going both directions.

Caleb found himself needing to barter for his daily needs. He began to trade for useful items and found himself occasionally

Tears on Frozen Ground

*Right: The spring.*

*Below: The brook, much like it appeared to Caleb in 1828.*

selling an item to a traveler. He added a shed for items he could pick up around the boat docks at Batesville and kept them on hand for these travelers. He had developed his little two-room home in the wilderness into a trading post without meaning to do so.

Sometimes he would keep two or three items of the same kind on hand. Bullet molds and powder were always in demand, as were harnesses and plows for workhorses. He kept a fire pit, anvil, and tongs on hand, along with some sledgehammers and blacksmith items. He was not a blacksmith, but he had observed other blacksmiths at work around Loudoun County. He knew he could learn some of the trade on his own. By 1829 he was doing okay for himself, at the young age of twenty-two.

Caleb had learned a lot about the Eastern Indians at his native home in Virginia. Caleb likely had some Indian in his own blood. He had learned some Indian dialect and could communicate with any tribe. This knowledge proved handy for Caleb around his homestead and trading post, as the eastern Indians often came through on their trek toward the new Indian Nation in the west. At times, Caleb was sought out to help interpret between whites and Indians. Bartering with a group of such Indians could easily have led Caleb Bales to his first wife in 1829.

In 1830, a census of Independence County was conducted. This census began in June of that year, with six months given to complete. In this census, Caleb is shown as living with a woman between fifteen and twenty years of age. Nothing is known of the young woman living with Caleb. She appears only as a checkmark on the census, with no name given.

It is believed that in 1832, this young woman gave Caleb his first child, whom they named Susan. Susan can be found on census records until 1850, at times living with Caleb and Jincy. Later, her name appears on census records from the Indian Territory of Oklahoma.

Sometime in midsummer 1832, Susan was born, and Susan's mother died soon after. Caleb's first spouse died at an early age, as so many did on the frontier, with no recorded explanation as to why they died or where they were buried. They so often just disappeared from history. Caleb buried her close by the cabin and the spring where he would spend the rest of his life.

On August 21, 1832, Caleb volunteered for one year of active duty with Bean's Rangers. This would have been to get away from the heartache of losing his wife and being left with a young daughter he had no idea how to care for. Details of his circumstances will likely never be known, which leads me to believe he left his baby girl with a neighbor family while he went off for a year of service with a company of mounted Rangers. It was not uncommon for other nursing mothers to care for a motherless child during these times. This frontiersman must have felt pressure to get his life and plans together. He also needed a companion or wife to care for young Susan and provide him with his future family.

Caleb Bales, along with several other young men from Independence County, Arkansas, saddled up their horses, loaded their saddle bags, and rode into Batesville to join Captain Jessie Bean's mounted Rangers volunteer group for a one-year tour of duty. The Congress of the United States had just approved, in March 1832, the President's request for six hundred mounted Rangers to assist with Indian problems. Some were sent to Florida to fight in an Indian war going on there, while others were sent to various places with similar problems. Caleb's Rangers of Bean's company (approximately 110 men) were sent to Fort Gibson in Indian Territory to help with the problem of new Indians coming into the territory and to help suppress the conflicts arising with so many different tribes in the area. Some of these Indians were at war with each other even before the official Cherokee Trail of Tears began, which was still another six years away.

Many Cherokee left the old Indian Territory in the 1820s and early 1830s. The encroachment of the white man and an earlier treaty offered some incentives for the Cherokee to move on west of the Mississippi; little did they know how difficult it was going to be in the Indian territory of Oklahoma. The Cherokee had given up making war earlier at the insistence of the Father President "to become civilized like the white people."

These Cherokees were now homebuilders, farmers, and teachers. They had forgotten their war parties and ways of war. Now they were on a frontier with several other tribes, and the other tribes were making war with each other. The Cherokee were at a huge disadvantage in war. Captain Bean's Rangers were to help bring peace among the Indians.

Caleb was known as a good interpreter between Indians and the English speaking military forces at Fort Gibson in 1833. His Captain Bean, who was in charge of the company of Rangers Caleb had just served a year under, was assigned to a group of the new Ranger replacement companies who arrived at Fort Gibson in August 1833. At the request of his former neighbor from back home, Caleb agreed to stay an additional three months to assist Captain bean in communicating with the Indians in the territory. This would also allow Caleb more time to find a wife and mother for young Susan.

# On the Trail Home

When his duty was over on August 21, 1833, Caleb found himself with a pocket full of money ($465.00), a good horse, a rifle, and a pistol. He was in a good position to barter for an Indian maiden. In western Arkansas, in what had just become Washington County, his future would become much clearer as you will see in my fictionalized account below of the first meeting of Caleb and Jincy. Most of these names, dates, and circumstances are recorded in history.

After hanging around the territory for a few months, Caleb had not yet found the wife he was looking for. He was not anxious to return home without a wife to help him with Susan and raise a family. He knew he was in no shape yet to undertake caring for a baby. But he knew he needed to go home. In early December 1833,

Caleb departed from Indian Territory in Oklahoma for the long trip back home to Independence County, Arkansas. Traveling the same trail he knew from his trip to Oklahoma the year before with Captain Jessie Bean's Rangers, he planned to spend the night at a camping spot they had used. As he approached this site, late in the day, he was surprised by a group of two dozen or more Cherokee and Choctaw Indians. They were guarded by a squad of U.S. soldiers. In this company of twenty-five or so Indians was a beautiful young girl who looked to be in her early twenties. This small group had been part of a larger party, but they had fallen behind due to sickness and injuries. Caleb caught the eye of this young lady. She was sitting on a log by a fire, cooking a pot of mush. She had a younger brother with her. They had camped at this small site for a day or two of rest before the final leg of their journey out of Arkansas. A few troops were at watch over these Indians, charged with delivering them from Tennessee to their new home in the Indian Territory. With his gear placed underneath a tree and his horse hobbled nearby, Caleb sat nibbling at some salt pork and observing this party of very poorly clad Indians.

Jincy spoke in perfect English when she invited Caleb to partake of the mush she was ladling out to her brother. Then she rose to her feet, and Caleb immediately saw she was moving with great difficulty. She managed the few steps toward Caleb to bring him food, showing courage and determination with each difficult step. Caleb could only rise from his seat and go toward her, offering help. He gratefully accepted the hot food and entered into conversation with this young woman and her brother. He soon learned that Jincy, the oldest, was eighteen, and her brother James was sixteen. They had left Tennessee with their mother and two sisters, but now there were only the two of them. Their mother had died on the journey and was left in a pile of brush alongside the trail close to the Mississippi River. One of her sisters, Polly, had been lost long ago on the trail, and her other sister was far ahead with friends and family in the main party. With everything so difficult, Jincy had offered little resistance when Sally was invited to travel with this family who also had children. Now she was also lost to Jincy, miles ahead in the main group. She now only had faint hopes of seeing her again in the territory.

Caleb learned that James was staying in Washington County to search for his lost sweetheart, who had come in an earlier group. Jincy would be going on to the new Indian Territory as soon as the orders were given. Jincy knew by now to follow the orders of the guards who were escorting them west. She had suffered harsh treatment from these guards. Time to camp and rest had been in short supply. The work assignment of these guards in charge would end as soon as they delivered this party of Indians to the new territory, and all were anxious for the end to come.

The weather had turned extremely cold across Arkansas in late November. Freezing rain, sleet, and snow had made travel almost impossible, but still the soldiers in charge had insisted on moving ahead. It was during this time that Jincy's feet became frostbitten. A surgeon assigned to the main party had removed several toes from each of Jincy's feet, leaving her crippled but alive. These Indians were poorly clad, with not enough clothing or blankets, and at the point of freezing, with sickness, frostbite, and death afflicting their party almost daily. They struggled to travel just six to eight miles a day. A healthy group with adequate clothing and food might make twenty miles a day.

The lieutenant left in charge of this struggling group called his staff of guards together and said, "We are at a good campsite with plenty of water and wood for fires. We have got to stop, rest, and let these savages build fires to warm with; otherwise we may lose them all." He then ordered them to "announce a rest period. Tell these Indians to build large fires and shelter themselves as best they can. We will rest a few days."

Upon hearing this announcement, the small group of stragglers came to the realization that their friends and loved ones in the main group might never be seen again. Days of struggling to gain ground had given them hope of rejoining the main group at a point up ahead. They had met and heard the stories of other wandering Indians on this trail who were searching every camp and settlement for lost children, wives, and parents, most never to be found.

The beauty of the young, crippled Cherokee tormented Caleb as he tried to bed down for the night. He not only felt sorry for her, but he also wanted to help her. She had very little chance of survival where she was going, especially in her hobbled condition. He had noticed that both of her feet were wrapped, and the wrappings were dirty and bloody, though Jincy made daily efforts to clean and wrap her feet, an almost impossible task in the daily rain, snow, and dirt of the trail.

After wrestling with this throughout the night and constantly looking in on Jincy as she tried to sleep with severe pain, his mind began to focus on the guards. He was determined to find the man in charge of this group. He could clearly understand that this group was lagging far behind the main body with little hope of finishing their journey anytime soon. He began to feel the possibility that his bartering skills might come in handy. He had already, upon seeing Jincy, wanted to take her by the arm and help her. Only his shyness had prevented him from doing so. He now knew that he must talk to this young maiden and seek her permission to try to help her by taking her off this trail.

*Would this move seem too sudden for her? Might she be unprepared for such invitation as to embarrass me in this camp? Would she be polite, understanding, and simply give me a quiet refusal?* All this was running through Caleb's mind as he took his blanket and approached the wagon Jincy lay under. Quietly, he spread the blanket over Jincy's shoulders, trying not to awaken her. To his surprise, Jincy was not asleep. She was trying to rest and stay as warm as possible with the heat from the fire and her own poorly clad body. The only cover she had was a shawl, barely large enough for her shoulders. Jincy opened her eyes slightly as she accepted this act of kindness from the Ranger. She could only offer a slight curl of her lips into a smile as a thank-you. Caleb backed away and placed another log on the fire next to the wagon. He spent the next several hours tending the fire to keep as much warmth as possible drifting toward and under the wagon.

*Who was this man?* Jincy had overheard the officers say he was a Ranger. She could tell that underneath the shaggy hair and beard was a man with compassion. He seemed to understand the terrible conditions that this party of Indians was exposed to. His kindness in placing the warm blanket over Jincy's shoulders had taken her by surprise and was such a comforting act that she felt a warmth that made her feel relaxed and grateful. She felt a need to rest in the comfort of the campfire and the warm blanket that had so graciously been placed upon her. She liked this man's personality and character; she now needed to take advantage of the warmth she felt and rest.

Her body and mind had been stressed to the limits for months now since that awful day Jake Hartwell and James came riding in with her daddy and brother tied across the back of two horses, murdered on their way home from the supply depot. She had lost so much since that last night in her home. Her mother had died on the trail, her sisters Polly and Sally were lost on the trail, and her brother was about to leave her. She was about to be alone and in no shape to even do the things necessary to survive in the new wilderness of the Indian Territory.

She would be at the mercy of others, and where she was going was full of wild men who would take her in to be their squaw. She prayed for better choices. Underneath the warm covers, she began to think of all she had lost in the last few months. Her losses would become overwhelming once her brother left sometime in the next few days. "Lord, help" seemed to be the only prayer she could muster, and the words of her mother echoed in her ears: "Jincy, stay the course."

Her mind drifted back to their last night together in early June…

*\*\*\**

*The farmhouse with its tall, smoking chimney and chinked log walls.\* Her siblings, George, James, and Polly, busily going about their chores. Little Sally playing with her doll. Jincy saw her momma as she stood in the doorway calling them in to supper. Papa was out by the well washing up after a long day of*

\*The italicized section is a dream sequence written by Diane Frie.

## Gale Maag

*cultivating the corn. Jincy admired him! He gave his family a deep sense of security and love, and there was no doubt how he felt about Momma.*

*"When do you think the corn will come in to harvest, John?" Momma asked.*

*"Oh, I reckon maybe a week," Papa said between bites of salt pork and biscuits. "It looks to be a good crop this season, better than last year. I need to take a wagon trip up to the supply depot in the morning. George, I need you to go help me with the load."*

*George Craig was the eldest at nineteen and an asset to his family. He had grown into a fine man with his father's sense of integrity and his mother's kindness. He would be married in the spring to Tollie Hartwell, his match in every way. What a fine family they would make!*

*Early the next day, Jincy watched as George hitched up the wagon. Papa and Momma stood next to the horses and talked in low tones. At times, Momma seemed close to tears, but she hid her feelings whenever the youngsters came close. Jincy knew something was not right, but she said nothing.*

*Papa held Momma before lofting himself up next to George on the wagon seat. One sharp slap of the reins, and they were on their way. George turned back to face Momma and called, "See you tomorrow," as they both waved goodbye.*

*Momma looked like a statue standing in the center of the dirt road. Jincy moved across the yard and clasped hands with her mother, as they strained to see the wagon disappearing into the trees.*

*Jincy looked into her mother's eyes. "What's wrong, Momma?"*

*Momma smiled weakly and patted Jincy's hand. "No need to worry, child. Papa and I were just fretting about the low price our corn might bring this season."*

*Turning to face her mother, Jincy pleaded, "I've heard the whispers in our village, and I know there's a chance we might all be going away. Please, Momma, are the rumors true? I'm not a child anymore. I'm seventeen years old!"*

*Modare Craig searched Jincy's eyes and recognized true strength in the face of her oldest daughter. She knew this girl was a child no more. She glanced about to make sure the little girls were not in earshot. Momma spoke in a tone that was hushed yet full of determination and honesty. "Yes Jincy, truth is, peril surrounds us on all sides, yet God will control our destiny. I need you and your brothers and sisters to hold fast to each other no matter what comes. Papa is on his way to supply us for an escape into the mountains. Many of our people are leaving and returning to the old ways of the Overhill Clan. We will join them."*

Jincy's family had lived like the English for as long as she could remember, so living in the old way would be quite an adventure for them all.

Papa and George had been gone for two days, and Momma was becoming more worried each hour. John Craig was nothing if not a man of his word, and he had told them he would return home the following day. He was a full day late!

"James, I need you to take a ride out to check on Papa and your brother," Momma said. "They are delayed too long, and I fear they are stranded with a loose wheel or some other trouble." Momma did her best to conceal her worry, but Jincy knew in her heart something was terribly amiss.

She asked a question that she was sure she already knew the answer to, but felt compelled to ask nonetheless. "Could I ride along with James, Momma?"

"No, dear, I need you here at home, I would like you to help James make ready for his trip," Momma replied.

Jincy helped James pack his saddlebags for travel that would certainly last overnight. She made sure he had food for himself as well as Papa and George.

James saddled up, then turned to Jincy. "If I'm not back by tomorrow afternoon, send Jake Hartwell to find us, and have him bring an extra horse." Jake Hartwell was George's betrothed's father and a very close friend to the Craig family.

"All right, James, I'll do it, but why?"

James lowered his eyes to the ground, then looked back into his sister's face, "Just please do as I am asking, Jincy."

She was overwhelmed with a sudden rush of dread! As James swung himself up on his horse, she reached out and grabbed his hand. They remained motionless for a long moment. James squeezed her hand, and without looking down, nudged his ride forward down the path. Jincy helplessly watched her brother disappear into the trees just as she and Momma had watched Papa and George vanish from their sight two days ago. All she could do now was pray the three of them would return safely.

The next afternoon came, but there was no sign of the Craig men. Jincy dutifully went to Mr. Hartwell's home and requested he go out to look for them just as she had promised James.

Night fell on the third day. Momma, Jincy, and the two younger girls were alone. All were in bed by dusk, but Jincy could not sleep. She dressed and slipped out of her loft bed, then went down into the fireplace kitchen. There she *found Momma on her knees, tears streaming down her soft cheeks, praying in silence for the deliverance of her family. She knelt next to her mother, and as she did, she was engulfed in her momma's arms. Both remained together until dawn, when they heard horses coming up the trace.*

*"They're back," Momma breathed as she hurried toward the door and rushed out to the road.*

*Jincy had dozed off just before her mother heard the hoofbeats of horses, so Jincy was several steps behind.*

*"Oh, Momma, they're home!" Jincy excitedly called out as she cleared the door, but the picture waiting for her as she reached her mother's side was not the homecoming she had prayed for.*

*James and Mr. Hartwell were mounted on their horses and leading two others behind. Draped over the horses were the bodies of Papa and George! Momma sank to her knees and held her hands over her mouth so tightly it seemed she would stop her own breathing. She remained still until James came to her. He helped her up, and tried to take her back to the house, but she would not budge.*

*With James still steadying her by the arm, Momma turned to Mr. Hartwell and asked, "Jake, what happened?"*

*Jake stood with his hat in his hands and spoke straight to Momma. "Near as we could tell, they were ambushed. It looked like they both put up a good fight, but they were outgunned. Whoever did it took all the supplies, the horses, and the wagon. Modare, John knew he was taking a chance when he planned to run; you knew it too. Our people are being murdered all over our own country every day! As for my family, we aren't going to resist any more. We are going to the territory across the great river; it's the only hope for happiness and freedom. I can't tell you how sorry I am for your loss." His voice was hoarse with emotion. "Now, I have to go home and tell Tollie."*

*Momma thanked him for being a true and honest friend, and as he rode away with his dreadful tidings to share, she turned her attention to her own sorrow. "Now I will see them for myself." She spoke in a voice so calm, it was troubling.*

*Momma righted herself, stepped away from James, and went to the first horse that held the body of George. She saw bruises on his face and the bullet holes in the back of his shirt. She remembered George as her darling boy who brought her wildflowers for her table. She saw the wonderful man he had grown* to be, and would grieve for him and for his chosen bride, Tollie. "He was a kind soul," she said as her trembling hands softly touched his face. She kissed his eyes, closing them forever.

Next, she went to Papa. Her steps faltered, but she caught herself against his horse. "Take him down, James," she said as she lowered her body to the ground and covered her head with her shawl.

James removed Papa's ties. She pulled Papa into her arms, ran her fingers through his blood-matted hair, and began to wail the mourning cry of the Cherokee. It was as if all time stood still, and Momma's cries reached into the very heart of God. An eternity passed before she gave out in exhaustion, and she allowed the men who had gathered there to take her son and her husband away for burial.

Jincy, James, Polly, and little Sally could only stand by and watch.

\*\*\*

English men came to the house and told Momma that Papa had sold the farm to a man named Jacobson. She was warned that the family was to move out fast. They even showed her a deed signed by Papa and witnessed and signed by several white men on the day of his death.

Momma pleaded for time to harvest the corn, and Jacobson gave her permission to do so, provided she gave him a share of the price she received for its sale. She agreed, and the whites left, seeming to be satisfied with their bargain. Within the week, the Craigs finished pulling the corn, and it was stacked and ready in their wagon.

"After we sell the corn, we will take the money with us and run to the mountains. My plan is to finish what Papa started. We will follow through and hide with the Overhill Cherokee. Be ready to leave at first light for market and from there to our new home," she said while serving their supper of venison and cornbread. "Eat quickly, then we will gather our provisions for the journey."

The sound of horses and shouts of angry riders cut through Momma's plans like a knife! Riders came up the trail and surrounded their home, shouting obscenities and waving torches as if to burn them out. It was Mr. Jacobson and his hired men, accompanied by two soldiers. Altogether, there were about eight men.

"Come on out, squaw, and make sure you have all your red stick brats with you!"

# Gale Maag

*Momma reached for the latch to open the door. She had barely placed her fingers on the handle when she was knocked to the floor by a burly farm hand crudely shoving his way into the room. A soldier who appeared to be in charge followed and ordered, "Git up, woman, and take your brood out o' here. Mr. Thaddeus Jacobson is now take'n possession of this here farm and all its buildin's, and ever thang in 'em."*

*James helped her to her feet as she tried to reason with these senseless men. "Please, let us gather some things for our own needs! We were not ready for this yet. Are our lives worth so little that you wouldn't allow us supplies to travel? No matter where we are going, we have common needs!"*

*Jincy and Polly were trying to grab clothing and food. Poor little Sally just clung to her rag doll and to Momma's skirt. James stood stoically by Momma's side.*

*"Out," screamed one of the soldiers, and he began shoving Momma along like a dog.*

*Jincy kept on gathering provisions, until the same soldier yanked her out of the door by her long braid and swung her into place behind Polly. "Take one last look at the good life, injuns. Your time on white man's land is over in Tennessee."*

*Jincy couldn't help it, even though she knew it would do her no good. At the end of the road, she looked back. The wives of Mr. Jacobson's farm hands were already running through the door to their house, and she could see the livestock being played with by their smiling children. She and her family had just lost everything, and the English were laughing!*

*"No matter what happens, the Lord is in the midst of it," Momma said. Her strength had always come from her faith. She had been converted as a child in the mission school and had transferred her belief to all of her children. "God never promised us our lives would be free from suffering, He only said we would be with Him if our faith stayed firm. The Lord has a plan; we just have to hold fast to each other and stay the course."*

*The girls huddled close to Momma as they settled in for their first night away from their home. They had reached the village where others were preparing for the long journey to the Indian Nation west of the great river. They made their beds there on the ground. Their journey to the west had just begun. Plans for Daddy and Momma to leave for the old ways and join the Overhill Clan were now lost along with everything else. They had no choice except to go west with the village and hope for help as they began the journey.*

\*\*\*

After Momma died on the trail, Jincy saw the shawl covering her mother's body through the bare-branched pile of brush.

"Roll her over to the side and cover her the best you kin. We don't have no time for grave diggin'," said the lieutenant.

Momma had died before dawn. She tried to share her warmth with her smallest child, Sally. Wrapping the same shawl around Sally last night, she had exposed her own body to the bitter cold Tennessee elements. Now, Jincy stood on the cold path and held tightly to her sister's tiny trembling hand.

"Get going," shouted a soldier, shoving his hand into her back.

She plodded along as if in a dream, and each step became heavier. Could it be true that this unrelenting, unforgiving, nightmarish march of sorrow began only two months ago? It seemed an eternity had passed.

"Jincy, I'm cold," Sally whispered. "When are we going to stop and rest? My belly hurts." Jincy's thoughts shifted back to the present, and she turned her face downward to look into her sister's wide dark eyes. Sally, who was only six, was so small and now completely dependent on Jincy's protection. Twelve-year-old Polly had been pulled from them one night weeks ago.

\*\*\*

*Momma held tightly to Polly as she slept, begging three drunken soldiers to leave her alone. Jincy watched in horror as they pulled Polly from her momma's arms and dragged her away screaming out of the camp and into the woods beyond.*

*"No, she's only a child! Can't you see that? Take me, please, take me!!!" pleaded Momma. She ran after them, only to be beaten down to the ground and kicked into unconsciousness.*

*Jincy raced to her mother and pulled her back to the fireside. Thankfully, Sally had remained asleep through it all.*

*It was morning before Momma regained her senses. Jincy went with her to the tents at the center of the camp where the officers were stationed. She told them what had happened, and they assured her that someone would "check into it."*

Gale Maag

*Momma prayed for strength to stay the course. Polly was gone.*

***

"Hop up to my back, Sally, and I'll carry you for a while," Jincy said as she knelt down to the ground. Sally climbed on and wrapped her arms around Jincy's neck. When the cold of her sister's arms hit her skin, Jincy realized she had made a terrible mistake. "Hide your face in my hair, Sally," she breathed as she slowed her pace. Lagging behind, she slipped silently into the bushes along the trail. Her feet fell quietly, even on the dry grass, as she retraced her steps. Jincy's focus was unwavering, until she reached her mother's brush-covered body. Gingerly, she stretched her hand and arm into the pitiful grave and gently pulled the shawl from her mother's face.

"Momma," she sobbed, "we need this for our journey." Her last memorial to her mother's dignity had been to reverently cover her lovely face. Even this respect would be denied Modare Craig at her final rest. Jincy held the soft cloth to her lips, kissed it, and glanced at her mother's face one last time before she turned to the task at hand.

Looping the shawl under Sally's bottom, Jincy tied it over and under her own shoulders to secure her sister on her back. She had seen her mother carry children in this fashion many times. "Try to rest, Sally," she whispered.

Muffled sounds of horse and harness coaxed her back to reality. The slow, plodding ribbon of women was just ahead, and no soldiers appeared to be watching as she stepped from her hiding place. Jincy thought her soft footfalls would be overlooked by the guard, as she silently merged from her concealed position along the path and back into line with the other women.

"Where you been, girl?" growled a voice from behind her. The lieutenant's disdain for the Cherokee came through loud and clear with every word he spoke. His lips curled back under his heavy brown mustache. "Looks to me like you've been grave rob'n'," he said as he walked toward the girls. The other women watched in horror and helpless desperation as the Lieutenant sized up these new targets of his cruelty.

Jincy lowered her eyes to humble herself and tried to keep walking with hopes this evil person might allow her one act of disobedience to pass unpunished.

Instead, the lieutenant's wrath fell on her like a hammer! She came to a violent stop when he grabbed hold of the shawl tied around her body. He jerked at the shawl until Sally tumbled to the earth, screaming in disoriented fear, and Jincy crashed down beside her.

Jincy turned to look at him and tried to speak, but no words were allowed to form on her lips. The last picture her mind registered was the butt of Phillips's rifle coming down to strike the side of her head…

Jincy felt the motion of the rocking wagon and struggled against the fog of dreams still veiling her coherent thoughts. She painfully opened her eyes, but the searing trauma did not allow her to keep them open. She forced her lids into a narrow slit and saw several elders sitting in the wagon with her. Sally was next to her talking, but the words were nonsensical. Finally, her mind focused, and she remembered the abuse she had endured at the hands of the lieutenant. The words falling on her ears became clear once more.

Sally was crying. "Jincy, I thought they killed you. Don't die like Momma. Please don't leave me, Jincy, please!"

Jincy felt Sally's tears fall on her face as she brushed her hair back from her eyes.

Sally continued, "You told me, Momma said we had to hold fast together, so you can't go!"

Jincy pushed herself upright and forced a weak smile. "Sally, I am not going anywhere."

When the lieutenant realized Jincy was coherent, he ordered the wagon to stop. "This one won't run off no more," he declared as he yanked her shoes from her feet. He grabbed her arms and dragged her past the others and tossed her back to the trail. Sally ran next to her sister. "Now we'll see how she likes walking the rest of the way in her socks."

Ice was forming a thin crust on the muddy river, a short distance from the town of Memphis. The lieutenant gave the order to camp on the riverbank for the night. He allowed the men to rejoin the women, but each had to search for his kin. "We ain't responsible fer family reunions," he said with his sickening, low laugh. They would cross the swirling, icy waters in the morning by ferryboat.

The girls gathered brush for a fire and settled in for the night, hoping James would come soon. They had been issued two thin cotton quilts, and they had Momma's shawl. Wrapping themselves together in the covers, they tried to rest. Jincy's head still pounded from the Lieutenant's beating, and her feet were beginning to ache from the cold because he had taken her shoes.

Her mother's voice whispered in her ear. "Stay the course."

Jincy couldn't allow Sally to see her pain. Her little sister had the determination of a mule, but this ordeal was more than any child should have to bear. She knew Sally was thinking of the dead they had left behind and was wondering where Polly had been taken. Polly was twelve and next to Sally in age. She and Sally looked alike with their long black hair, willowy build, and fine facial features. Polly was tall for her age and carried herself proud and straight. The Cherokee were not short, stocky people like so many natives. They tended to be taller with fine, sharp features and almond shaped eyes. Polly and Sally were two who possessed the best of these traits. Polly was coming into young womanhood, and her beauty was that rare kind only given to a few. Momma had the same natural loveliness, but hers had turned softer with age. Jincy could see Polly's beautiful, sleeping face pictured in her thoughts, as she dreamed of their last night at home.

***

The group of travelers stopped at a small settlement called Oil Trough. James went quickly to start a campfire. The weather was terribly cold, and it had been snowing for most of the day. He knew his sisters would need to warm up fast. His concern was even greater for Jincy than it was for Sally. Jincy insisted on carrying Sally on her back with Momma's shawl, which gave Sally more protection from the cold. James piled up gathered brush and started a fire. He unloaded their few supplies from his own back, then turned his attention to his sisters. "Now, sit down, girls, and Jincy, let me check your feet."

Jincy unwrapped the worn quilt strips, saying, "They really don't feel too bad. I don't feel them much at all now."

James looked on in disbelief at her darkened toes. He had never seen frostbite before, but he was pretty sure this was it. "Can you feel this?" he said as he pinched her toes one by one.

"Ow! Only my big toes. I can't feel the rest. What's wrong with them, James?" Her voice was shaky, and he could see the fear on her tired face.

"I'm going for help. You stay still. I'll be back soon. Sally, you take care of her, and don't let her move." James walked from one campfire to another until he found a soldier hitching his horse for the night. The soldier had a kind face and said he would do what he could for her.

The young cavalryman returned with James. When he saw Jincy's feet, he could only cover his mouth with his hand and whisper, "Dear Lord! I'll go find Doc Rowland. We got a lot o' sick injuns right now, but he needs to see this." He smiled at Jincy and said, "Don't you worry none. Doc'll take good kere of you." As he turned to leave, he pulled a whiskey bottle from his blue coat and handed it to James. "See she drinks as much o' this as she kin before I git back with the Doc. This ain't good. She's gonna lose those toes."

James went back to the fireside. "Jincy, you have to drink this, as much as you can. The soldier was a kind man, and he's bringing help. I've heard the others talk about the doctor, and he is someone to be trusted."

"Please, don't make me drink this. It smells bad, and it will make my stomach churn. Why do I need it? Tell me what's going to happen, James. Nothing could be worse than what's already come to us."

James put his hand on Jincy's arm and squeezed it gently, then looked at Sally. "Come on now, walk with me. You are going to sleep at our neighbor's camp tonight. I'll come get you in the morning." He took her by the hand and led her away but returned a few minutes later. He knelt in front of Jincy and said with as steady a voice as he could muster, "Jincy, the doctor is going to have to take off your toes. If we don't do this, you could die. You need to drink the whiskey to help with the pain."

Jincy's face paled as she looked at her feet, then back at the bottle of amber liquid. Without a word, she raised the bottle to her mouth and took a swig, then another, and another. The taste was worse than she expected, and it burned something awful, but she kept it down.

Doc Rowland introduced himself to James. He examined Jincy's feet and explained as best he could what he was going to be forced to do. "She's got some bad damage. All the toes on her left foot and four on her right have to come off. There's even damage to part of her left heel. I'll try to save as much skin as possible, but she won't be able to walk for a while." His face darkened with his next statement. "The Lieutenant will be told that she has to be put in a wagon."

He reached out to James and handed him a metal instrument with a long, thin handle. At the end of the handle was a flattened, metal crescent. "Pour some of that whiskey over the end of this, then put it in those hot coals. When I say so, hand it to me quick." Lowering his voice and leaning closer to James's face he said, "Boy, she's sleeping right now, but as soon as I start, she's going to come alive. We may need another pair of hands to hold her down. You want to fetch help?"

"Yes, I see the soldier who brought you to us. I'll get him, if he's willing." James walked outside the warmth of the fire to where the young man stood. Concern filled his eyes when James asked for his assistance, and soon they were both with the doctor, making ready.

The kind-faced man knelt down beside Jincy and spoke softly to her. "My name is Sam Cole. I'm gonna have to hold you down a mite whilst Doc here works on your feet. He says it's gonna be tough, but I know you'll be right as rain."

Jincy stirred and opened her eyes. "I remember you. You're that nice man who smiled at me. No one seems to smile at me anymore. That was real kind of you."

"She's very full of spirits, Mr. Cole," said James, a little taken aback by his sister's drunken chitchat. "Please don't take offense at her being so familiar."

Sam looked back over his shoulder at James. "Not to worry. Poor little thang didn't deserve this. She got treated cruel for no good reason. Some of us wanted to stop it, but we got outranked. It's the least I can do."

Doc Rowland turned to his surgical kit and poured whiskey over his instruments and his hands. "Time to start, boys. James, use a piece of cloth to hand me that cautery when I call for it. Sam, take hold now."

Doc wasted no time. He picked up a small, saw-toothed knife and made quick work of Jincy's toes. As each toe was removed, he called for James to hand him the red-hot iron. Doc placed it over the end of each bleeding stump to sear the wound shut, then rinsed it with whiskey, and James placed it back into the coals. He repeated this process on both feet until all that was left was the big toe on her right foot. He took off the damaged skin from her left heel but was pleased to see it was not as badly frozen as the toes. A few horsehair stitches were required at the stump of her left big toe and on her heel, but nowhere else.

Jincy's vision was blurry, but she could see Doc Rowland wrapping her feet in bandages.

Jincy turned her gaze back to James and searched her brother's face for truth. "James, will I walk again? Did he take all my toes? I can't tell! I'm not hurting."

James spread Momma's shawl over Jincy, then moved her head into his lap and stroked her hair. "Pain will come with the healing, little sister, but now you will sleep."

James told her what she had lost in the surgery, and what she had not. She had not lost her life.

***

Jincy was wakened by the sound of a log being added to a fire. She felt both the warmth of the fire and the blanket that the Ranger had put on her last night. She had rested well for the conditions here on the trail. Now she had to get up and prepare some food for herself and her brother. Their breakfast would be leftover mush from the night before. The Ranger had already opened his bag of salt pork and was sharing some with James as she approached him from behind and placed the warm blanket around his shoulders. She liked this Ranger; he was kind and thoughtful, much different from others she had encountered lately. As Jincy hobbled back to a seat on a log by the fire, she gave thought to what she would encounter in the days just ahead. She had lost her momma and Polly on the trail, Sally was with another group miles ahead and might never be heard from again, and James was about to leave in search for his lost sweetheart.

Jincy would be alone out here in the vast regions of the west, and in her condition she could not even take good care of herself. So many of the Cherokee were in similar situations, with lost family, little food, no homes, and cold weather.

Makeshift shelters would hastily be erected for a little protection. She doubted she could make a shelter on her own, and she had no one to go forward with. She would be dependent on others to provide food.

She had thoughts of settling near the government agency that had promised assistance during the first year of their entering the new territory. Thoughts of becoming the squaw of a wild Indian in the territory brought fear to her. She was educated and respectable, and now she had only her faith to carry her on into the unknown of what lay ahead. She prayed for happiness and family—a family of her own and a husband to grow into old age with.

***

As for Caleb that fateful night, Jincy's kind acceptance of the blanket convinced him that he must be patient and learn more about this young woman. Tomorrow would be a new day. He was anxious to learn all he could of her and her brother before those in charge might decide to move on. He might only have a day or two. He closed his eyes, trying to rest as he turned over thoughts in his mind. What would tomorrow bring? Then, for the first time that night, he thought of his little Susan and home, then drifted off to sleep, resting against a tree only a few steps from the fire. The next morning, as he shared some salt pork with the young woman's brother, he was surprised when a warm blanket was placed across his chest and around his cold neck. He was more warmed by the smiling face of Jincy as she turned away and hobbled back toward the wagon.

Several people were stirring and trying to warm themselves around the fire Caleb had kept going throughout the night. Old and feeble people were climbing out of the wagon. Some needed help to get to the ground. They seemed to be pleased that they were not required to prepare for travel on this cold winter day. But Caleb sensed that several days rest would not adequately prepare this group for the tough trail that lay ahead. Some looked very much like they could not live through another day, on or off the trail.

Lieutenant Phillips told Caleb that the group had left Ross Landing in late September. They traveled by boat up the Tennessee River until they reached a part of the river near Rudd's Ferry that was too low for navigation. After several days of camping alongside the river, the decision was made to strike out overland. There was a trail to Memphis, and on the word of a government agent, the captain was able to purchase a few wagons to help continue the journey.

This group comprised an entire village of Cherokee who decided to flee the area after the encroaching white men made their lives miserable along the busy travel route the white men used in search of land. Along the way, the guards had also picked up several more Choctaw Indians to make a sizeable party of approximately two hundred people, and the guards were to deliver them to the territory.

The group made it to Memphis by mid-November and camped near the Mississippi River. The need to find even more wagons and provisions for the completion of their overland journey caused further delays. The crossing of the river at Memphis that followed was a brutal experience for everyone in the group.

Author's note regarding Lieutenant Phillips's story:

In 1831, Alexis de Tocqueville was visiting Memphis when these escorted Indians arrived on their way west. De Tocqueville was a French diplomat, political scientist, and historian. In his best-known work, *Democracy in America*, he wrote of what he saw in Memphis:

"The wounded, the sick, newborn babies, and the old men on the point of death... I saw them embark to cross the great river and the sight will never fade from my memory. Neither sob nor complaint rose from that silent assembly. Their afflictions were of long standing, and they felt them to be irremediable."

Jincy and her family could have been with a party much like these Choctaw. They crossed at Memphis on a line west that would take them into a country where Batesville was known as a large trading post. De Tocqueville's account took place only a couple of years before Jincy and Caleb met. Indians had been coming into Arkansas in large numbers long before the 1838 Trail of Tears. It's hard to imagine how difficult this relocation was on these people. These Choctaw completed their removal to the West under army guard.

Since the captain of the party containing Jincy chose to travel overland from Memphis to the Indian Territory, they were now departing for Batesville, Arkansas. Between Memphis and Batesville lay several miles of low, swampy lands. Once they made it to Batesville, the hilly terrain to the west would make for better trails. The captain hoped to reach the territory by mid-December and conclude the journey.

Travel across the swampy forest of eastern Arkansas proved to be much more difficult than anticipated. Trails were almost invisible, and camps were often in cold, wet areas where no comfort could be found. Mud made it difficult to get the wagons through,

## Tears on Frozen Ground

and travel slowed to only a few miles daily. The Indians grew even weaker. The guards were short-tempered and showed less and less patience. They pushed to cross the swamps, often becoming sick themselves from the inhuman conditions along this trail.

Finally, the group of weary travelers found themselves on the banks of the White River, just below the busy trading post of Batesville. The Indians were allowed to build large fires and rest while the captain made arrangements for supplies and repairs. They would camp here for a few days.

Ice, rain, and snow brought about the beginning of the brutal winter of 1833-1834. Traveling upriver in a northwest direction, the full blast of the winter wind seemed to always be in their faces. The creeks and rivers were frozen with ice, the banks always muddy just under the soil's frozen crust. Frostbite became a daily torment and had to be treated. There was so much pain and suffering that some with frostbite let it go undetected and untreated along with their other pain. (Such was the case of our Jincy.)

As the number of sick increased, any space in the wagons had to be used for the very weak and elderly. Travel slowed from twenty to twenty-five miles a day to ten to twelve miles a day, and still Indians were reaching the camps well after dark, unable to keep up during the day.

The captain called his lieutenants together and advised them to split up the group. The healthy would go on ahead to the territory, and the sick would be brought up behind. He felt that he must get those healthy enough for the remainder of the trip moving forward before more sickness struck. The decision was made to hold back all those who were sick and crippled, along with a few family members to help care for them. There would be enough healthy family members to provide wood for fires and prepare meals to keep this lagging group moving along. The forward group would make haste for the territory before winter conditions worsened, as was expected in the west. The separation occurred in mid-December 1833.

Lieutenant Phillips was a tired, worried, and sick man himself when preparations for this separation were made, and with his own health in mind, he had been quick to volunteer to lead this struggling group.

Caleb listened to the lieutenant tell this story and realized that this man would eagerly give up any or all of these Indians to rid himself of the misery associated with this command.

***

Now that Caleb knew that he could bargain for Jincy without difficulty, he had to approach Jincy and her brother James with his thoughts. As he went to the wagon, he was greeted by James.

James was interested in discussing with Caleb the territory that lay ahead. They were near Washington County, Arkansas, the place where James had hoped to find his sweetheart from back home in Tennessee. It had been several months since he had seen her or any member of her family. They had left their homeland almost undetected for fear of being persecuted by members of Chief Ross's tribe who believed the Cherokee should not leave their homes. James had seen her briefly the day before they left. She had promised to wait for him somewhere in western Arkansas, just before entering the Indian Territory. James wanted as much information as he could get about the trail ahead and any villages and settlements where he could begin his search. Jincy was going on to the territory with hopes of reuniting with her sisters, but James had little hope of ever seeing them again. The trail was full of Indians with missing relatives, and very few were ever located after being separated in the vast areas of the wilderness.

Caleb shared with James Granville Craig what he knew about the territory. James would forever be grateful to Caleb for the information. James later found and married his sweetheart, and they had several children. Their line can be traced in the archives of genealogy. James also named a son Caleb after his friend from the trail.

***

As the second night approached, Caleb and James engaged in more conversation about the territory James was going into. Jincy bedded down, much like the night before, just underneath the wagon and as close to the fire as she could, to get relief from the bitter cold. Again, Caleb took his Army-issue blanket and spread it across Jincy's chilled body, and again she accepted his warm gesture with a smile. Caleb and James continued their conversation well into the night, occasionally putting another log on the fire. Finally, Caleb leaned back onto his tree, and with his saddle for a seat between him and the cold ground, he drifted into sleep.

Caleb woke before the others, just as the sky was beginning to turn grey in the east—the way home. Caleb wanted to go home more than ever since his departure. He wanted to see Susan, and more than anything, he wanted to bring her home a mother. He now knew who he wanted that mother to be.

Jincy was also awake, and she walked toward Caleb with the blanket that had kept her warm throughout the night. Caleb was on his feet as Jincy held it out to him, thanked him, and turned back toward the fire.

"Wait," he said.

Jincy stopped, and before she could turn around, Caleb placed the blanket back around her shoulders.

"I'm making you a gift of this blanket. Keep it around your shoulders and body all the time." He added, "You will need it."

Then, in a moment of boldness Caleb had never before experienced, he said, "I want to take you off this trail. I have a home less than two weeks travel from here. I need help and will take you for a wife, with your permission."

He could not believe what he had just said to this beautiful maiden. He stood silently and waited for her response.

Jincy could only stand there. She had prayed daily for someone to care for and to have children and build a home with, to help take care of Sally. Suddenly, tears welled in Jincy's eyes. Her frayed shirt was the only thing she had to wipe at the tears with. Her shoulders shook as she silently wept.

Caleb didn't know what this meant. He was sure she had no husband—only her brother and a sister far ahead. Why was she crying? Had he hurt her? James came to her, not understanding why she was sobbing. No sounds of crying came from her mouth—only the shaking of her shoulders and the tears flowing and now dropping from her cheeks and onto the frozen ground gave away her crying.

Her beautiful facial features were wearing thin after so long on the trail. Jincy might have given up and died except for her love for little Sally and her brother James. Now Sally was gone, and her brother was about to go try to find his sweetheart, lost from him somewhere in western Arkansas.

Caleb, standing silent, didn't know what to do.

"What about Sally? I can't leave her." Jincy spoke in a tone soft and clear. "I can't leave her." At the same time, Jincy knew that she had already lost Sally. She was somewhere miles ahead, with a good family to adopt her.

Caleb, with unnatural boldness, reached and took her tear-wet hand. "I have a one-year-old at home with no mother. Maybe you can adopt her. With you helping me, I can provide for us all."

Jincy's first thought went back many miles on the trail to Sally's tearful eyes when they had lost their mother. She looked to James as if needing his approval.

James said nothing—he too was stunned by this conversation and what was so suddenly taking place.

After a few moments of quiet and thought, James walked up to Jincy and put both arms around her, and they embraced like they never had before. "The God we pray to for happiness and direction has found favor in our prayers." He paused, again thinking, *we have suffered so much, we have stayed the course, and now we must receive the blessings God is giving to us.* Still pondering this scene, James spoke again. "Dear sister, I will find Sally somewhere ahead. If she is in need, I will return her to you, and if she is happy, I will tell her of you and your blessing and also tell her where you are. She will always know where you are and will find comfort in that. Pray that I might also find the same answers to our prayers here in our new homeland. Yes, sister, go, and go with my blessing."

She slowly turned, facing Caleb, hobbling toward him with her arms outstretched, and he met her halfway. They embraced warmly.

"Caleb," she said, in a warm, quiet voice, "I will help you, I will love your child, and if the Lord is willing, give you many more. We will do it together, and more than anything else, I will love you."

Caleb was so shaken by this response he could not speak. Words were difficult to form in his trembling mouth, but finally he spoke. "Jincy, if the Lord is willing, we will give this beautiful country many children and grandchildren." Then he added, "I will be patient with you, and I will be true to you. I will take care of you and help you overcome the scars of your past. I will provide for our future offspring and I will love you, so help me God."

With this said between them, there on a cold winter morning in western Arkansas, a covenant was made. Life was taking a good turn in both their lives. Difficulties lay ahead and they would face them together, a rock for each other.

As they disengaged from their embrace, Jincy once again pulled Caleb toward her. As Caleb leaned to her, she kissed him on his bearded cheek. "We will do well, Caleb Bales; it's God's promise."

Caleb had little trouble bartering with the lieutenant for Jincy's release. An agreement was quickly made, and the lieutenant was thankful to be rid of one more problem. Jincy would never know what Caleb paid for her freedom, but she would always be grateful.

By midmorning, Jincy was seated on Caleb's horse, and she and her brother were saying their last goodbyes—he going to search for his sweetheart and Jincy going to her new home in Independence County, Arkansas. They would never see each other again, but history from the very heart of the Cherokee Nation and then throughout the entire world would reveal thousands of their descendants.

***

Author's Note:

It is not known for certain if James ever found Sally; however, a Sally Craig is listed in the archives of the Cherokee Nation. Her adoptive family must have safely delivered her through the journey, just as many, many children were by other adoptive families on the trail.

Polly was never heard from again after being abducted and lost early on the trail. No record of her has ever come to my attention.

***

Caleb, with the reigns of the horse in his hand, turned off to the east and down the trail. Jincy turned in the saddle to give one last wave to James and never looked back again. She was going home.

On December 30, 1833, the two of them entered a rooming house at Batesville, Arkansas, tired, ragged, and worn. Here they would take shelter for a day's rest. Jincy slept on the bed with Caleb on the floor nearby. Tomorrow would be a day for buying a buggy and winter supplies so they'd be well prepared for the remainder of winter in their cabin home nine miles north of Batesville.

Caleb was pointed to the office of Dr. Jonathan Isom as they departed for their first shopping spree this cold Tuesday morning, December 31st, 1833. Caleb and Jincy found the doctor to be a kind, soft-spoken man. They both appreciated his inspection of Jincy's feet. He, after hearing the story of how she had lost these toes, was very descriptive in how she should treat them and also found some clean white rags in a dresser there in his office, and in a short time he had her feet doctored with a soothing ointment, which he packaged up for their trip home. He explained to them both that she was extremely fortunate that there was no infection in her feet. The ointment was enough to get them completely healed over, and the rags he sent with them were enough to wash and have clean rags daily. They had made their first new friend. If and when they needed medical services again, they both were satisfied with Dr. Isom.

Caleb paid cash for the doctor's services. Then they left, still with several chores to do, Jincy riding on Caleb's horse to the mercantile store for the purpose of buying winter supplies of food. They would also buy a few clothes at this store. The last thing Jincy asked Caleb for was a Bible, as hers had been lost back in her old homeland during their evacuation.

Jincy would go on to be the spiritual leader in her family, reading Bible stories to her growing family and then answering their questions. She would also teach others to read from this Bible, just as she had been taught back home in the Blue Ridge. They were then well prepared for the remainder of winter in their cabin home nine miles north of Batesville.

The rest of the day was spent shopping for little items needed for winter in the cabin, then a bath and one more night of rest in the rooming house. They departed Batesville on the first day of January 1834, heading north, both warmed and rested after so long on the trail by the two comfortable nights at the rooming house. Jincy looked beautiful in her new, plain dress that she would remember forever as her wedding dress. Caleb also looked handsome with his neatly trimmed beard and haircut, and in his new clothes and hat.

Caleb and Jincy had agreed to be married on the first day of the New Year—a new beginning to a new life. As they traveled the road north from Batesville, Caleb knew where he must stop first. In just a few miles, he pulled up to the home of James Davis. Caleb and James had ridden their horses into Batesville sixteen months ago and joined the mounted Rangers. Caleb was sent west with Captain Jessie Bean's Rangers to help restore order in the Indian Nation of the Oklahoma territory. James was sent off to Florida to fight in the Seminole Indian war there. James Davis, Justice of the Peace, joined this couple together in holy matrimony there in his home on January 1, 1834. Later, James would file these papers at the Independence County courthouse, where they still remain to this day.

***

Just down the road and around the bend, Jincy began to see the valley Caleb had told her about. From the hillside, she could see the small cabin with a chimney reaching toward the sky and the silhouettes of the cottonwood trees along the bank of the little brook and the spring where she and Caleb would spend many happy hours in the years to come.

The meadow around the house was full of life. As they approached, quail flushed and startled the horse. Jincy was reminded of her home in Tennessee that sat back near the forest; she could almost hear voices drifting up the road, such treasured memories of the hills where she was raised. The sun was setting as they reached the cabin, and when her injured feet touched the ground, she paused to recognize the song of a whippoorwill down in the valley. Jincy was home.

Now a married couple, Caleb and Jincy knew there was another place to go in the morning. Little Susan was just down the road, and this was to be the first challenge of the newly married couple's life together. Susan was a happy little twenty-month-old and would not allow Caleb or Jincy near her. She had the woman she considered her mother there next to her and Susan would remain with her adoptive family for the next several years. Her daddy Caleb could never establish a relationship with Susan that would satisfy her, even though she did occasionally spend time with them. She would remain forever in a fractured relationship with her father, a casualty of the times.

***

Jincy's recovery from the harsh treatment she had undergone on the trail was slow. Her feet were steadily getting better, but she would forever be crippled due to her missing toes. Thoughts of the harsh treatment of the guards on the trail began to diminish. She had started on the trail in early fall when the trees were just beginning to show the brilliant foliage as they do each year. She and James had departed their homeland with 182 Cherokee, including women and children. Some of the menfolk had gone on the year before to try to establish homes for their families. After being on both the river and the trail a few weeks and then heading into

## Tears on Frozen Ground

western Tennessee, they were joined by twenty or so Choctaw. The government, which promised to see them safely to their new home in the territory of Oklahoma, felt the need to send the last of the Choctaw along with these Cherokee to be moved west.

The Choctaw were a beaten-down and demoralized group of Native Americans, stripped of all their worldly possessions except for the few things they might carry under their arms. They joined the Cherokee without any hope, completely submissive to orders from the guards. Getting along with the Choctaw was no problem—they all seemed hopeless, and traveling was, to them, without purpose except to receive a ration of food and water twice a day.

Now as Jincy was recovering from her own broken spirit and physical health, she became more and more thankful for the things surrounding her here in this remote area of the frontier. Caleb was seldom away for more than a few hours at a time, and she could always expect him home for supper, well ahead of the frightening nights. Jincy still had issues of trust with the white people, still fearful of another night like the last night that she and her family had in their Cherokee homeland. Caleb was often assuring her that things were to be good for them and their family from this point forward. Jane, as Caleb had grown to call her, was slowly accepting her new surroundings.

Housework was light for Jane during the first years of her marriage to Caleb. There were only two rooms to their cabin, and it didn't take her long each day to straighten their house. Normally, by the time she finished her chores in the mornings, she also had a pot of something cooking on the fireplace. Later in the day, she would often fix cornbread that would last for several meals. As soon as she was caught up, she was out the door looking for Caleb, leaving her pot slowly cooking there on the fireplace.

She was always anxious to find Caleb out near his blacksmith shop, where he bartered with items needed by others in the area or with travelers coming through. Travelers were a common thing here on the trail between Weavers Chapel and Batesville, which points northwest to Sandtown, Melbourne, and Calico Rock.

If no one was around, she and Caleb would often walk down the few steps to the spring where Jincy did her washing. This spring was also their constant supply of cool, sweet water for their home and a wonderful bathing spot during the hot, humid days of summer. The bottom of the brook that had the spring at its head was covered with large boulders that had been lying there for thousands of years. The rocks, some as large as a house, had smoothed out over the years and offered a great place for them to sit and let their feet hang into the large pool of cold water.

Caleb had designed a small piece of iron, made in his shop, to be a gate there in the bottom of the brook, just a few steps downstream from the mouth of the spring. They could place this piece into a slot of rocks and fill the pool with water. When the pool was full, the water would reach a point where it was diverted and went around the pool and on down the brook, uninterrupted, to Polk Bayou, leaving the pool full. He had also chosen a spot that would be hit by sunlight, naturally warming the water during the day for a nice bath at day's end. Jincy and Caleb used this pool almost daily in hot weather. Very few people during this time had a place for a daily bath, especially one so easily made ready. It was known as their secret spot and was hidden from view until you were upon it. The gate was stored in late fall and not used again until the warm sun of an early spring day made the water so inviting.

Jincy and Caleb spent much time together at the stream. It was beautiful in the shade of the cottonwood trees. Much of the spring was so shrouded by the trees that it was in total shade until autumn frost, when cold weather stripped the trees of their foliage. A better place to rest at the end of a hot day was not to be found. The events of the day were often the topic of conversation here in the cool surroundings of the spring.

Even today, the beauty of this spring can be enjoyed, and except for some noticeable pipes pumping water from the spring to supply a human-made pond, it is exactly as it was in 1834, with the smooth, inviting shape of the rocks, the shade overhead, and the sound of running water.

## Tears on Frozen Ground

*\*\*\**

Jincy's life with Caleb became better with each passing day. Caleb had been very patient and protective of Jincy since they had met on the trail, when she had been so frail and weak from abuse. She was getting stronger, slowly putting the nightmares of past events and of her mother's death behind her. The loss of her sisters was still heartbreaking for her, but she had been able to put this in the past as well, as if it were a bad dream.

She and Caleb had begun talking about raising a family shortly after getting married. She had learned to love Caleb and what he had done for her on the trail the day he bartered with the lieutenant for her release. Now she wanted to give Caleb children and raise a family. But for some reason, she had been unable to conceive a child. This tormented Jincy, as she knew how much Caleb wanted more children; he already had plans for a larger home next to the present one.

Caleb had begun early in their marriage to place the cornerstones at the site of this future home. He calculated the grade of the places to set them, leveling them, and placing them in just the right places. A few logs had been pulled to the site and every calculation was made to erect a four-room home with a large attic that would serve as a bedroom for their children. A breezeway through the middle of the home on the main level would offer a place to relax and listen to the sounds of early night for years to come.

Caleb's plans were that of a caring husband and father, but the few logs he had prepared were beginning to age there in the yard of their future home. It was plain to both Jincy and Caleb that the larger home was unneeded without a larger family.

Caleb continued to protect and provide for himself and his wife. They spent every spare minute they could find together by the spring, sometimes bathing together and sometimes just letting the cool water rush across their tired feet. They went hand-in-hand, as Caleb always felt he should help Jincy across the uneven steps leading into the center of the brook. Jincy walked much better now that her feet had healed, and Caleb would help her walk when she needed it. He loved to help her—it showed his love for her, and he would continue to do this for their entire married life. Jincy accepted his help, for she knew what it represented.

It was here at the spring, one beautiful, warm fall day in the late afternoon that Jincy told Caleb she was pregnant, four years and almost nine months after they had married. She had wanted to tell him weeks ago but waited until she was absolutely sure. Caleb was so surprised and emotional that it reminded Jincy of the time she said yes to his marriage proposal.

In April 1839, Jincy gave birth to their first child, a son whom they named James Allen Bales, after Caleb's good friend, who lived up the road and who had married them that New Year's Day five years previous.

The next spring Davis Bailey Bales was born. Then in the following year, Jincy gave birth to another son, Francis M. Bales. He was followed by two girls, Dianna Mason Bales in 1843 and Minerva J. Bales in 1845. They were followed by three more sons: Willard Filmore Bales in 1848, Willis Bruer Bales in 1849, and John Benjamin Franklin Bales in 1850. Finally, their daughter Celia Isabel Bales was born in 1851.

Celia was to be the last of Caleb and Jincy's children. From all these children, their grandchildren and great grandchildren number into the thousands today. My mother and dad alone had over one hundred and thirty in our family tree when my mother died in 1997. The number is still growing rapidly.

***

Jincy was a caring mother to all her children. Between April 1839 and April 1851, twelve years to the month, she gave Caleb nine children. We have no record of any child dying young, as so many did under similar conditions during this time in history. Undoubtedly, she used medicines from roots and leaves to help protect these children as they grew, things she had learned from her own upbringing in the Indian Territory of the eastern states. She was an amazing woman, passing along all sorts of wisdom to her children. She taught them to read and write as she had taught others in the mission school before she was moved west. She was also a spiritual woman, as she had been taught earlier in her childhood. This alone had much to do with her will to live and protect others.

Now, more than one hundred and seventy-five years later, we all imagine what it was like for this frontier family living in the remote wilderness of Arkansas.

\*\*\*

It seems that the very soul of Jincy is in touch with us, even today. We know Caleb and Jincy are buried there on a hill a short distance from the spring. Exactly where, we may never know, but they are there.

\*\*\*

From the front porch of the log home, there by the spring, Jincy pointed the boys to where she wanted Caleb's grave on the hill when he died on September 15, 1862. They also marked a place for Jincy there beside Caleb, and she died one year later in 1863.

Jincy's death was brought on mostly from the grief of losing her Ranger, the one who had bought her off the trail thirty years prior. God had provided her all her dreams and prayers. Children, grandchildren, and a wonderful home there on the frontier, but most of all a husband to love and be loved by, her Ranger, Caleb. She wept daily for his hand, then thanked God for all the days and years she had it.

# Notes

My great-grandfather was James A. Bales Sr., the first child born to Caleb and Jincy Jane. He was born in April 1839 and died in 1915, only a mile from his birthplace. He was buried at Hickory Valley in an unmarked grave.

James A. Bales Jr. was born at the home of his parents, James and Mary Ellen Lewis Bales, on June 28, 1863. He married my grandmother, Margaret Angeline Marshall Bales, on November 21, 1895. They also lived with James Sr. at his home on Cave Creek Road for the first several years of their marriage, until 1903. They had four children while living with the senior Bales'. James Sr. also had a trading post there on the road in front of their home.

In 1903, James Jr. built a three-room log home a short distance down the road from his father and moved his family there. A drawing of this home is on the cover of this book. Mom had told me years ago what the house looked like, the number of rooms and the detached kitchen on the back. This picture was drawn by my sister Ramona Maag Yates from Mom's description.

Hester, the fourth child of James Jr. and Margaret, was born on October 18, 1901. She was thirteen years old when her grandfather, James Sr., died in 1915. She knew her grandfather well, and the story she told us of Jincy Jane being crippled in both feet to the point she could not wear shoes was one she heard from her grandfather, who was Jincy's first child.

My cousin Jo Sykes Chesser revealed to me that her mother, Dorothy, told of her grandfather James Sr. calling her his little Indian Princess. Dorothy was seven when her grandfather died.

As for Hester, she did not reveal many stories about her relatives. This was probably because she was not given a lot of information, as all of her parents, grandparents, and even aunts and uncles were trying to lose the identity of "breeds." Mom never told me that her father and grandparents were Cherokee. I believe this was an unspoken truth that was never discussed.

# Epilogue

Descendants of Caleb and Jincy have searched for years for the burial place of these two settlers. Most searches centered around Weavers Chapel Church, located about eight miles from downtown Batesville. Because the church is about two miles from the spring where Jincy and Caleb lived, people guessed Jincy and Caleb might be buried there in the small cemetery next to the church in unmarked graves.

Word of mouth suggested they were buried on the original home place in unmarked graves. This bit of information created a curiosity and the search began.

Members of my family have spent many hours and road trips into the very heart of Independence County trying to solve the mystery of our missing grandparents. My son Stan, grandson Ben Adams, and I explored all over the area in 2012 and met a distant cousin, Ethel Dowell. Ethel was near 100 years old when we met. She was very receptive to telling stories about our common great-great-grandmother Jincy. At one time during our conversation, she reached over and took my hand in both of her hands and said, "Her blood flows through both of us." Stan and Ben were in awe at the bright personality and charm of this old lady.

*Ethel Bales Dowell, who was nearly 100 years old when my son Stan, grandson Ben Adams and I first met her. None of us will ever forget meeting this charming lady. Ethel is shown here standing near the spring and in the likely area of Caleb and Jincy's cabin.*

She introduced us to her daughter who lived next door, Barbara Carpenter. Barbara had information as to who now owned the original property. A valuable bit of information.

# Gale Maag

My nieces Jamie Fowler and Judy Owen spent a day with me early in our search; we gained knowledge during all visits. This visit was in March 2014.

In April 2015, my nieces Jamie and Pamela, along with my daughter Jennifer, Stan, my wife Peggy, and I spent two days searching. Jamie and Pamela flew in from New York, and Jennifer flew in from Wichita, Kansas. We tromped all over the hills surrounding the original home site of Caleb and Jincy and found an abundance of chiggers and ticks. The most important thing we found on this trip was the meeting of Vaughn and Neva Brokaw. Vaughn, a direct descendant of Jincy and Caleb, was still living there close to the original home site. He and Neva were very welcoming to us and our search. They opened their beautiful home to us. They were the special part of this trip; we all left with love for this couple. I wish my entire family could have known the Brokaws. This acquaintance would eventually lead us to the actual site of the spring and the graves of our Caleb and Jincy.

Our distant cousin Vaughn had bits and pieces of information still stored in his weakening mind, and he shared what he could remember with me. Vaughn was a grandson of Mary Comer and a great-grandson to Matthew R. Comer and Dianna M. Bales Comer. He still had a faint memory of where his ancestors were buried on the original homestead. He tried to explain to me where the graves were, and we searched the area but found nothing. These searches were over a period of time that extended into two years.

In 2016, Stan and I scheduled a visit, and with the approval of Vernon Cummings, the owner of this property, we brought an all-terrain vehicle that we could use to tour the property. Vernon met us at Weavers Chapel, and then we picked up Vaughn at his home. Both of these two older men were well-acquainted with each other and with the property and the area of the spring, as well as with the old road that went to Sandtown. (This road now dead-ends at the spring.)

We, the four of us, looked at the land from the comfort of the vehicle. Vaughn and Vernon both enjoyed the tour as neither were able now to walk a tour. Late in the tour, we approached an area a

Tears on Frozen Ground

*Right:* Neva Brokaw, about to hug Stan Maag, who is greeting her with his hand on his hat (upper right). Jennifer Maag Adams looks on.

*Below:* Vaughn Brokaw, bidding us goodbye from his and Neva's mountaintop home. Mom (Hester Bales Maag) was born at the bottom of this mountain on property owned by James A. Bales, Sr. Vaughn, our distant cousin, would eventually remember and lead us to the Comer Cemetery.

short distance from the spring and Vaughn remembered a small family cemetery located there in the woods where five or six people were buried. Vernon also recollected the same. Vaughn stated that it was called the "Comer Cemetery." This statement really aroused my interest.

Matthew Comer married Dianna Mason Bales, daughter of Caleb and Jincy, and together they raised a large family on this very same property. This bit of information stirred my interest as I remembered a picture posted by someone in our distant family of the broken tombstone of a Matthew Comer. This would become the name of the forgotten cemetery here in the remote forest of Independence County, Arkansas. Stan and I both walked to the location these two men pointed out and almost immediately recognized an area that looked like sunken earth where graves might be.

We both made mental notes of the location and returned to the vehicle. It was now getting late and we had to leave. These two gentlemen, especially Vaughn, had a wonderful look at places they had not seen in years. It had been many years since he had seen the spring and property that lies in such a beautiful valley which at one time was occupied by many members of his family. He was overjoyed at seeing this one more time.

Shortly after this tour, he and his wife Neva were forced to leave this area for the comfort of a nursing home in Batesville. They were no longer able to live alone away from their health care providers.

Stan and I and another of my sons, Kelley, made another visit to Batesville to see Vaughn and Neva at a very nice nursing home there in that city. We were pleased to see them still very alert and close to each other.

A year passed before I scheduled another visit to the area close to the spring.

***

*Gale Maag, sitting at the spring on the very rocks where Caleb and Jincy spent time.*

## Saturday March 4, 2017

The events that happened to Stan Maag and me today were almost unbelievable. Exciting, satisfying, and spiritual would be some ways of describing the events to unfold to us this day.

At 8:30 am on this Saturday morning I drove Stan and I into Batesville, Arkansas. We decided to stop at McDonalds to have some breakfast. We parked, and before exiting the car I called Vernon Cummings, the owner of the original Caleb Bales property there close to Weavers Chapel, and informed him that we were in town. He knew in advance that we were coming, and in less than an hour we were following him onto the property, which is approximately nine miles north of downtown Batesville.

We visited with Vernon for about two hours there in and around his cabin on the hill overlooking the very spring where Caleb and Jincy spent so much time in the years of the 1830s, '40s and '50s. Vernon tired after a while and left us alone to try to discover the burial sites of our frontiersmen ancestors.

Stan and I drove down to the woods where we had a year earlier thought they might be buried. Upon arriving there we were somewhat confused as to just where we thought the graves might be, Stan thinking they were to the right and I thinking they were beyond this site and farther down the valley. We both got out here and began to search for what we a year earlier had thought might be unmarked graves. I was still unsatisfied that this was the correct spot and left Stan there searching, got back in my truck, and went on down the valley a short distance.

After looking over the site where I thought they were, I decided that I was in the wrong place and went back to where Stan was. About thirty minutes had gone by the time I parked the truck again and walked out to join Stan in his area of the search.

As I made my way back to Stan, I observed him almost frantically searching and jabbing the short metal probing rods we had. These rods were only about three feet long and would not penetrate very deep into the ground.

I walked over to where he was, and as I approached he was softly saying, "Okay, guys, show me where you are." In prayer he was speaking toward the ground where he was standing. When I got to his side, but not until I got to his side, he stuck his probe to the ground, just below and between where we were standing and immediately felt something underneath the dirt and leaves. He raked off the leaves with the end of the probe, and we immediately saw a piece of rock appear from underneath with lettering on it.

"There it is," he said.

Then we both went to the ground and began to uncover a tombstone with "Matthew R. Comer, husband of Dianna M. Comer" engraved on it. We were both elated. We spent the next hour cleaning and discovering the small headstone of Dianna Mason there next to her husband.

Stan and I were excited as we discussed Dianna Mason Bales, this daughter of Caleb and Jincy's. It has been told down through the years among our relatives that Dianna and Matthew were buried next to her parents on the original Bales home place.

Tears on Frozen Ground

*Right and above, left: Stan and I found this small cemetery containing five or six graves.*

*Above, right: Mathew R. Comer, husband of Dianna M. Comer. He was a blacksmith by trade, which would have been very useful on this frontier homestead. He died at a young age of forty-four years.*

Gale Maag

As we were sitting there basking in the seventy-degree weather with the sun pouring through the bare, leafless trees, we noticed a truck coming around the bend in the lane leading to the hilltop cabin. The truck was at first thought to be Vernon coming back from a rest. However, this was a different truck. It looked like Vernon's from a distance, but as it got closer it was obviously not Vernon.

Two men got out of the truck and approached us through the woods, calling out, "What's going on?"

I called back, "We are having a picnic here."

"You pick a heck of a place for the picnic."

"We are particular about where we picnic," was my response.

He laughed and introduced himself as Billy Cummings.

I asked him if he was related to Joe Cummings.

He told me that Joe Cummings was his great-grandfather who lived back up the road two miles on Cave Creek Road in the early 1900s. Then he added, "It's strange you would ask me about Joe Cummings. Just a short while ago, I was with my father, Paul Cummings, at the hospital here in Batesville. His wife, my mother, is ill." He said, "My father brought up Joe Cummings and the good life he lived here in the area. Joe was well thought of and often helped his neighbors when there was trouble. He was a good man."

As Billy continued on with his story, I was all ears.

"Dad said that one time around 1904 Grandpa Joe walked through the woods, a distance of some few miles, to fetch a doctor at Cave City to come out and treat a young girl who had just gotten burned badly when she caught fire from a wash kettle in the front yard of her home, which also was a short distance from Grandpa Joe.

"Dr. Gray from Cave City came out in his buggy to attend to this little girl and instruct the mother on how to daily treat her badly burned body."

I was dumbfounded as I listened to this man tell a story that was 113 years old and about my mother.

This old story is significant enough to be told again in 2017, at the same time in history that Stan and I were looking for the remains of her ancestors. Billy had just left his father after hearing this story and came to me and Stan. This man and I had never met; he had no idea who I was, nor I him.

I told Stan later that if we had sent out a message for someone to come get us out of here it might take days to find us. Yet this man came right to us. And what a story he had to tell, and it was almost word for word as Mama had told it so many times in her lifetime.

At the time of the accident, it was not known if Mama would live. She did live, ninety-three more years, endured many hardships, and came out thankful to God and smiling. She was Hester.

Just before Billy left Stan and I at the gravesite, I asked him if he knew his great-grandfather Joe Cummings was seven feet tall.

He said, "No, I have never heard that, and we have no pictures of Joe."

Stan took my phone, and in just a few minutes, Billy was looking at pictures, on his phone, of the Joe Cummings family, taken around the turn of the century (1905-1910). I had gotten these pictures earlier from Vernon Cummings, Billy's uncle; however, Billy had never seen pictures of this man and his family.

He left with three pictures: one of Joe, another of Joe and two grandchildren, and the family photo. Billy's last comment to me when he left was, "The Lord sure does work in mysterious ways."

*The Cummings family, about 1915. Joe, the seven-footer, is obviously on the right, back row.*

## Gale Maag

He was going to show these pictures to his father, Paul, who had just a short time ago the same day shared the story of the young girl being burned.

As you can see in the pictures, Joe Cummings appears to be just what others said at that time, a seven-footer. Joe was not only a "good man" as Bill stated earlier in this conversation, he was a giant in the community. He was also the one who may have saved Hester's life at such an early age there on Cave Creek Road.

Over the years I have heard Mama speak of the Cummings family many times. They were a household name around the Bales' dinner table. I find them just as endearing even today, more than a hundred years later.

Needless to say, I had trouble telling Peggy this story when I arrived home; emotions of the day were still running high. I wish all my family could have been there.

# Acknowledgements

Special thanks to my sister, Ramona Yates, for her sketch of the old home place on the cover. To Jamie Fowler, for always directing me forward. Without her, there would never have been my first book, *Jack Dale*, and for her suggestion that Lolly Walter take over the editing and publishing of this work. What a great piece of advice! To Lolly, for enduring all my mistakes and correcting them. She had a way of understanding what I wanted to tell and getting the grammar right. I am no writer, but I have been told that I'm a pretty good storyteller. It took Lolly to make it sound and look right.

A very special thanks to Diane Maag Frie. She has spent hours upon hours developing her stories that are inside this cover. Her discovery of "Notes from my Memory" was the single most important bit of information I ever received. It led me to literally years of research in forming this bit of history of our beloved Grandmother Jincy Jane Craig Bales and Grandfather Caleb Bales.

Thanks go out to the owner of the original Caleb Bales homestead, Vernon Cummings, and also to his nephew Bill Cummings. I have been given access to this property for several years while developing an understanding of life during this period of time in American history. I was never denied permission to go there.

Thanks to a distant cousin, Barbara Carpenter, for directing me to the Cummings family and also to Vaughn Brokaw, a wonderful man who at the time was still living less than the length of a football field from where Hester (my mom) was born.

Special regards for another cousin, Ethel Bales Dowell, Barbara's mother. At near 100 years old when we met, she extended a warm greeting to me, my son Stan, and my grandson, Ben Adams, that is never to be forgotten. I can still feel her small hands surrounding mine as she talked about our Jincy. Stan and Ben were next to her, as close as they could get, so as to not miss a word out of her mouth.

To all my family that encouraged me and even visited these parts of Independence County, Arkansas with me, thank you. My sons Stan and Kelley; my wife, Peggy, and daughter, Jennifer; my grandsons, Reid Maag and Ben Adams; my nieces, Judy Owen, Jamie Fowler, and Pamela Milam: We all searched and searched for clues to this family history and created memories that might never be recorded.

## About the Author

Gale Maag resides in his hometown of Paragould, Arkansas, along with the love of his life, Peggy (Boyd) Maag. Paragould is not far from Batesville, another small Arkansas town, where many of the events of this book take place. Gale is an avid golfer, fisherman, and hunter. But more than this, he is a keeper of the flame of his family's heritage as well as the greater American heritage shared by so many families whose ancestors were here in America before this nation began. The strength and fortitude of his ancestor Jincy runs through his blood.

This is Gale's second book. His first book, *Jack Dale, The Life and Times of an Unforgettable Coach*, was a successful memoir chronicling the impact of the life of Gale's high school football coach.

Made in the USA
Coppell, TX
26 September 2020